I0727899

Ocean's Bride

DEMELZA CARLTON

DEDICATION

In memory of Peewee, a caged bird who
learned too late the price of freedom

One

"Your tea is ready, Tuan."

I blinked and the shadowy figure in the doorway departed, the sound of her footsteps fading.

William's arm tightened around my breasts as he pressed harder into my back. "Mmm," he sighed. "If only I didn't have to work today, I could stay in bed with you all day, lass."

Maybe this was the heaven Merry's church

priest had spoken about. The sheer joy of waking up beside the man I loved and knowing how much he loved me in return. Maybe not, too, for simply lying beside him reminded me of what we'd done last night and what I ardently desired to do again.

"It's not day yet," I responded. "The sun hasn't risen, so it's still our wedding night."

He chuckled and the bed creaked as he sat up. "My day starts before dawn, lass. I need to find out what news the wireless station received while we were busy in bed."

"We're still busy in bed," I insisted, reaching for him.

William caught my hand in his and lifted it to his lips for a kiss. "A good wife obeys her husband and a good husband earns his keep so he can support a lovely wife like you. Tonight, lass." He rose.

A good wife. A good, human wife. How could I ever manage to be that? I'd spent my childhood learning to lead mermaids and seduce humans. That made me a good lover, certainly, but a good wife? I'd never spent more than a night with the man I loved. Giuseppe had died the next day and William…William had… "The last time we shared a bed, you rejected me in the light of dawn, William. That night the ship sank and it was too late. I'm afraid…" I heard the weakness in my voice and stopped speaking. The ocean would not take him from me again.

William gathered me in his arms. "If I'd known what would happen, I'd never have left. I was angry at myself for giving in to my desires, for taking advantage of a girl I'd sworn to protect. I thought I was protecting you by leaving. You don't know how sorry I am."

I pulled him onto the bed beside me and settled firmly in his lap. "Then make amends, William. Now."

He stroked my hair. "If I can, I will. What can I give you, lass? My heartfelt apologies, a promise to never take advantage of you again, a vow to protect you always? I'd give you anything for you to forgive me for what I did to you that night."

I laughed gently. "It's not the night I regret, but the morning. All I want from you is what I wanted then."

"Name it, lass, and it's yours."

I shifted in his lap so I straddled him as I had his Triumph last night. Ah, but he was hotter and harder than the leather saddle as he slid smoothly inside me. "I want to take you for another ride, William," I sighed, tilting my hips to take him in deeper.

Two

I sponged perspiration from my skin with the tepid water in the washbasin, wishing I could go for a swim instead, until William's reflection in the mirror diverted my attention. He kissed my damp neck, smiled at me and whispered that he'd be back for breakfast as soon as he could.

"You'd better get dressed first, though," he called cheerfully over his shoulder as he left.

Sighing, I rummaged through my trunk for a light summer dress. I left off my stockings and shoes, choosing to pad barefoot along the floorboards to the kitchen. Idly, I wondered what sort of jam they had for my toast in a tropical climate like this one.

The kitchen didn't smell of yeast, like Merry's had on baking days, but that didn't deter me. William's cook had made tea for him, so perhaps yesterday had been for baking and the bread was stored somewhere. All I had to do was find it…

A large pan stood on the stove, and curiosity drove me to lift the lid. I almost squealed in delight at the sight of nasi goreng kampung, a fried rice dish I hadn't seen or smelled since I left Cocos. I hunted through the cupboards for a bowl and a spoon. The first piled-high spoonful set me to coughing, as I'd grown unused to the strong spices while living with Merry and her mild cooking, but the flavour of home was irresistible. I dug my spoon in again.

"Nooo, Mem, nooooo!" a woman's voice shouted.

Shocked, I found myself on one side of a tug of war for my bowl of rice. One of the serving women from last night had grabbed it almost out of my hands and it was all I could do to keep my breakfast from tipping out.

"Men's dinner. Not for you!" she scolded, slamming the lid down on the pan's contents.

I released my grip on the bowl, finally understanding. "You mean this is not for William and I? I'm sorry, I didn't realise. Here, let me help you make some more." I hurried to the cupboard where I'd found the uncooked rice earlier. I had no idea how to cook the stuff, but I'd learned from Merry that most cooking was along the same lines – follow the standard instructions and then flavour to taste. I grabbed a mixing bowl and dropped to my knees.

"No, Mem." She slammed the cupboard door, narrowly missing my fingers. "Breakfast at eight. Tuan's orders." She waved her hand at the basket of eggs on the table. "Not your place, Mem. Your tea is in the dining room."

No, not my place, I reflected and retreated to the dining room. The taste of chili still burned my tongue, so I poured a cup of tea from the tea service on the sideboard. Steam from the muddy brew wafted up and I knew I couldn't bear to drink it. I searched the room for an alternative, but there wasn't even a jug of water this morning.

William and his muddy, mine tea that no sane person would drink, I sighed, taking my cup back to the kitchen. I set it carefully on the counter and announced, "This is not my tea. This is for William."

She stared at the cup, then me in consternation. "I will make more, Mem."

"Maria. My name is Maria. Please, what is your name?" I asked.

"Cook. I am Cook."

I shook my head. "Not your job. Your name. It feels so impersonal to call you by anything else."

"Impersonal is good. Name is for family. In this house, I am Cook." She nodded at the other woman I recognised from last night. Her hair was still pulled into a tight bun. "This is Amah. She will take care of your children." She eyed my midsection. "Give Tuan strong sons."

Sons? I wanted to laugh. Boys were so rare among our kind that I'd never known one to bear a son. Human fathers couldn't sire sons with the people of the ocean's gift. No, the father had to be one of our own kind – a dragon, as my grandfather had been. But if bearing children was what good human wives did, then I could at least give him daughters. Perhaps humans were not so different to my kind.

Cook – if indeed she insisted that I call her that – seized a tin I recognised as the English style tea that William and Merry drank. Surely there was something better in the house. Chinese women didn't drink the foul English brew.

"Do you have any other tea?" I asked. "That

stuff tastes horrible. In Cocos, and in Australia, I didn't drink this."

Cook stared at me again. "Cocos? You are a Ross?"

She knew Cocos, for she'd named the family that ruled the islands. I needed to tread carefully. "No. My father was Wood-Jones. A cable man." A cable man who'd married one of the Ross girls after I was born, I thought but didn't say.

She nodded slowly. "My brother's family lives on Cocos. Working hard for your family, as I do for Tuan here. I will cook Malay food for you, Mem, if you wish. But Tuan…not for Tuan. He orders food from his faraway home."

I managed a smile. I'd forgotten William's inexplicable taste for flavourless food. "What I want is tea. Real tea without milk. Where is the tea that you drink?"

Cook smiled. "I will have Amah bring you some in the dining room. Tuan will have eggs and toast for breakfast. I will…prepare the same for you?" Her eyes strayed to the rice pan.

"Today, yes," I responded. "I don't want to steal someone else's dinner. But tomorrow…can you make more nasi goreng? Living in Australia, I've missed it."

Cook nodded. "Would you like Cocos eggs, or English ones?" she asked suddenly.

"Cocos."

"Yes, Mem." She grinned. "Eggs good for baby."

A baby? If I bore William a child, I'd be free of my banishment, allowed to command my own destiny. Mother would leave me alone. And it meant more time in bed with William, attempting to fall pregnant.

"Give William an extra egg, then." I nodded at the basket. "He'll need his strength if he's to give me a child."

Amah shot a questioning look at Cook, who translated my words into a language I didn't understand, but the other women did.

Amah smiled broadly and nodded.

Wonderful. We were all in agreement. If all I

had to do to be a good wife was convince William that we should make love at every available moment, I could manage. After all, I'd managed to pass for human in Fremantle with no worries.

But somehow, I suspected it wouldn't be as easy as it seemed.

Three

I inhaled the steam from my third cup of floral-scented tea, recognising the fragrance of jasmine from Merry's garden. This wasn't my preferred Japanese green tea, but it came in a close second as my favourite drink.

"Thank you, Amah."

I opened my eyes to see William striding into the room. Amah scurried away with his coat and hat. William poured a cup of tea and added a liberal quantity of milk before he sat in the cane chair beside me.

"Kiss me, Maria, or I'll swear you're still a ghost."

I'd barely set my cup down before he enveloped me in his arms, starting a passionate kiss that I didn't want to end. He pulled me from my seat and I climbed willingly into his lap, our lips not parting for an instant. His hand slipped inside my dress and cupped my breast, making me want to take the damn dress off and everything else, too, just to feel his skin against mine again. "William, oh William…"

Abruptly, his hands weren't touching me any more and he cleared his throat. To my surprise, he was blushing.

"What? Why did you stop?" I demanded. It certainly wasn't because he didn't want me – I could feel his arousal under me.

"Thank you, Cook," he said, not even looking at me as she set his boiled eggs and toast on the table. The smell of spices and soy drew my attention to the other place setting, now occupied by a saucy-looking omelette that smelled divine.

She smothered a smile and left, her shoulders shaking with laughter.

William gave me a gentle push. "We're the authority here. You need to behave properly. You can't just sit in my lap like one of the women from the White House. What will the servants think of you?"

I rose and smoothed my dress before settling into my own chair once more. "They think I'm your newly-wed wife, madly in love with you and eager to have a baby. Not as eager as those two are to see me pregnant, though." I nodded in the direction of the kitchen. "When I tried to make my own breakfast earlier, your cook almost tried to drag me out of the kitchen. It's not like I was going to set the place on fire. I learned to cook a passable meal during my time in Fremantle. Though nothing as good as this." I cut a slice of my omelette and popped it into my mouth. "Ooh, little prawns! She really did give me

Cocos eggs."

"What in heaven's name are you eating?"

I laughed. "Breakfast, William. The way they make eggs at Cocos. You can try some, if you like." I held out my fork and he eyed it suspiciously. "I trusted you enough to let you feed me chocolate. At least you know this is food."

He relented and took a tiny bite. I watched the play of expressions across his face. First surprise, then deep concentration, followed by puzzlement before he finally swallowed. "It's…tolerable, I suppose. Stronger flavours than I'm used to. And the shrimp are such an odd combination with egg. Not something I'd customarily have for breakfast." He swallowed a mouthful of tea. "Is this the sort of thing you ate for breakfast in Australia?"

"No. Merry made this delicious mulberry jam and I'd make toast in the wood stove in the mornings, just so I could have some of her jam. I had the timing just right so that I could make my toast and eat it in the time it took for the kettle to boil for tea before I went to work…" I drifted into silence as I saw the hurt tightening William's eyes. "I would have asked you to tea with me in Fremantle if you'd acknowledged me there. Instead, I had to follow you here. Maybe I could write her a letter and have the next carrier boat bring it to Fremantle for me. Perhaps she'd be willing to send us some jam as a wedding gift. She's the one who urged me to follow my heart, even if it meant traversing the whole ocean to find you."

William opened his mouth to respond. He no longer had the hardness he'd armoured himself in only moments before – this was the man I'd loved on the *Trevessa*, who'd spilled his heart to me in the Grotto.

"More tea, Mem?"

I glanced up at Amah and nodded, watching her pour the jasmine tea into my cup before thanking her. No tin mugs here – I had a fine china cup and saucer, like Merry had used back in Fremantle. I lifted the cup to my lips and regarded William over the rim. In my moment of distraction, his armour had returned, more prickly and impenetrable than ever. Inwardly, I sighed.

When Amah left, William seemed too intent on eating his own breakfast to talk about mine any more.

I laid a hand on his arm. "William, I lived as a respectable widow in Fremantle for seven years. I know how a woman should behave in your world. But I was born in a remote colonial outpost much like this one and you know that. In a population this small, those in authority set the tone for behaviour. And I am no one's subordinate."

"Lass, this isn't the tiny community at Cocos, or even the rough town of Fremantle. Truth be told, it's a cut above what I was used to at home in Scotland, too. We're the upper class here and we have to behave accordingly. It's as alien to anything you're used to as English was to you on the day we met. You're going to have to forget the life you knew and learn a whole new set of rules, all over again. Think back to when we met. What happened to the frightened girl on the *Trevessa*?"

I met his searching look squarely. "She took a moment to shake herself and remember who she was, and what she wanted. That was you, William. And she was willing to do whatever it took to win and keep you. Then and now. I knew I wanted you, and no shark or deranged madman or shipwreck would take you from me, not while either of us draws breath." I inhaled deeply, following his gaze to my swelling breast. "I will do whatever I must to stay at your side here. To be…to be a proper wife to you. How about you show me around the island a little today while you're working? Something like the tour of the *Trevessa* you took me on. And I'll show you I do know the proper behaviour even for a place like this."

"And if you don't?" William looked worried.

I grinned. "Well, I understand there's plenty of work at the White House for women who know how to please a man. I figure if I can please the man they call Grumpy McGregor, I shouldn't have much trouble at all."

His jaw dropped and he looked horrified. So much for my attempt at humour. "I'd sooner confine you to the house than that. If you can't carry yourself as an upper class wife here on the island, I'll have to keep you here until the next ship docks, then send you back to Fremantle."

Locked up and then banished, far from William? Not on my life. "It's a madman indeed who tries to cage a dragon against her will, even if the dragon is his wife." I rose and touched my lips to his. "Don't worry, William. I know to wear a hat and gloves in public. Not to mention shoes. I'll be the soul of propriety, I promise." And human, or as close as I could be. The way to be a good wife was not to be a dragon at all.

Four

When I'd finished my breakfast, I excused myself to go find some shoes. After a quick glance in the mirror, I sighed and resigned myself to a slightly longer time getting ready. I pinned my hair up and secured my hat with no less than four hat-pins. I grabbed my gloves and a pair of suitable shoes, biting my lip as I considered the stockings I'd avoided before breakfast. I rejected them again, clunking shut the lid of my trunk before I could change my mind.

I stared at my reflection, knowing it would receive Merry's nod of approval if she could see me now. Me, a demure housewife who drank her tea out of a cup and saucer. Tea made for her by a servant, as though I lacked the ability to make my own breakfast. Perhaps this was something William couldn't do, I reflected. After all, I'd known him on a ship, where our meals were prepared by a cook and stewards. I'd rarely seen men preparing food in Fremantle – always, it was the womenfolk who did it. Now he had me, I could change things. Cook and Amah could go and help some other deserving bachelor, leaving William and the kitchen to me. Perhaps he'd be more comfortable with only the two of us in the house and he wouldn't reject me for fear of what other people might think. Was desiring one's wife a weakness?

"You look beautiful," William said over the clop of my shoes as I descended from the veranda. He gave a nod and an Indian man took off on his Triumph, his tightly wound turban not budging at all as he opened up the throttle and accelerated.

I reached William's side, noticing for the first time that what I'd thought were crab holes in the garden exhaled gusts of air that smelled of the salty sea below. No crab could do that. Not crab holes – sinkholes into the caves beneath the island. No wonder Dubhan's cave had been so well aerated – he'd undoubtedly had many air holes to the surface, hidden in the jungle.

William offered me his arm and I took it, feeling the heat of him through his shirtsleeve and my white glove. Home. With him, I felt like I was home. Not in the watery world at Cocos where I'd spent my childhood…but here.

We strode down the road together, the mud fighting me every step as it sucked at my shoes or tried to help me slide a little faster down the incline to the cove. If it weren't for William's steadying arm, anchored by his heavy boots, I'd have slid into Flying Fish Cove on my muddy backside, I was sure of it. But when we rounded the final bend, I stopped dead of my own accord. The cyclone I'd swum in so happily had destroyed the port.

Hearing William's despairing description of the damage in the security of the Grotto was nothing to seeing the devastation with my own eyes.

The storage sheds beside the White House were smashed to kindling, flattened as though some huge creature had stepped on them and squashed them flat, while leaving the brothel intact. One of the piers was missing altogether – swept away by the storm swell that had raged where the calm waters rippled now. Not the triangular one where the *Islander* had unloaded, but the short one beside it where I'd seen the phosphate ships loading.

"Was anyone hurt?" I asked when I managed to find my voice.

William's eyes held sympathy. "No, by some

miracle everyone was fine. Even when boulders came down the cliffs." He pointed at the inland cliff where brown cascades of mud and rock had tumbled down the hundred-foot precipice, turning it into an incline of sorts, though an impossibly steep one.

I drew in a sharp breath. Landslides. I knew he'd mentioned them, but never had I expected they'd be so big. Some of the rocks sticking out of the mud looked bigger than Tony's truck and when I imagined the speed at which they'd hurtled down the cliffs to the land below…William was right. It was one of Merry's miracles that no one had been hurt.

William headed unerringly for a two-storey building that seemed to have taken very little damage at all, as it towered over the wrecked storage sheds. I climbed the stairs and froze when I reached the top and saw past the wrecked port to what had been the group of workers' houses known collectively as the kampung — the Malay word for village. The pier wasn't missing at all — the swell had strewn it along the beach, smashing it against palm trees and leaving bits on the eroded bank that had once been the kampung road. No more – the waves had washed away the road and the foundations beneath the rail line. From the debris washed up on the kampung verandas, it looked like the waves had licked the houses themselves. Between the landslide behind and the swell pounding their front doors, it seemed the ocean had truly tried to swallow the kampung.

I glanced at William, whose expression had hardened at the sight of the cove. He'd said it was his curse that had caused the damage. As if one man could call a cyclone. Not even one of the ocean's gift could call down a storm of this magnitude. Though if I'd been so inclined, I could have worked with the waves to destroy the other piers…

Think human, not mermaid. I shook myself and said softly, "It's not your fault, you know. The ocean doesn't curse people. It was just a storm. A bad one, but nothing out of the ordinary for this part of the world."

"It was the worst storm on record at Christmas Island. How is that ordinary?" William snapped.

I wondered what sort of storms my grandfather had experienced here, and how humans had survived on the surface then. "How long have humans been living on the island?" I asked absently, then held my breath as I realised what I'd said. I should have said people, not humans.

William didn't seem to notice my slip. "Forty years, give or take a few. The worst storm in forty years!"

"The worst storm to reach a tiny rock in a huge ocean in only forty years? And no one died? William, that's no curse – that's good fortune. I grew up at Cocos and it's a far different story there. We saw storms like this every summer, and sometimes more than once. I remember when I was a little girl, one cyclone levelled every building on Home Island. There were so many palm trees floating in the lagoon, along with planks from the houses, they could have made a raft big enough for the entire Cocos population." The raft William had found me floating on had been constructed from washed up cyclone wreckage – I'd watched the children lash it together and take it on short voyages between islands, before I'd stolen it in a fit of fury at my mother, my people and anyone else who was allowed to remain at Cocos when I was cast out.

William's voice cut through my bitter thoughts. "That must have been terrible for you. How did you survive, lass?"

On the raft, I'd survived on sheer fury alone until I'd succumbed to despair at my exile and the loss of all those I'd known and loved. When the *Trevessa* had spotted me, it had been days since I'd last been able to force myself to sing up a meal. But William wasn't talking about my banishment. What was his sympathy for?

The cyclone? I'd been all of three years old

and my sister had taken me into deep water to tumble in the swell, giggling together as we let the power of it carry us home. Duyong had taught me to ride the waves better than even dolphins could. Until Mother had found out and scolded us both. Ah, more painful memories and William was still waiting for a response.

I shrugged. "I was very small. I only remember that the houses were gone and it seemed all the fish in the ocean wanted to hide under the floating wreckage. There was food aplenty for weeks."

His expression seemed to hold awe. "It's a wonder you're still alive, given all you've been through. You're a survivor, that's for sure. I only wish I had your courage." He stared out to sea, blinking furiously.

What? William had courage in spades. He'd waded fearlessly into fights without showing anything but his certainty of a successful outcome. "I'm stubborn, not brave, William. It took a lot of courage to try to come after me in shark-infested waters when the *Trevessa* sank."

"If only I'd had your stubbornness then, I might have done more than try," William said darkly, then cleared his throat. "Come on, let's choose the film for tonight's cinema showing. Your choice, if you'll come to the cinema with me."

They had a cinema on this tiny island? "Of course! I used to go to the cinema in Fremantle with Merry or Tony. Well, I only went once with Tony. He took me to see this film about monsters that drank blood. *Dracula*, I think it was called. You wouldn't call me brave if you'd seen me then! It was a dark night with no moon and the cinema's outdoors, so you hear all sorts of noises, and then a frightening film to boot…ooh, that was the last time I went to the cinema with him!"

William's eyes blazed as he grasped my wrist. "Who is Tony?"

I didn't understand his anger. "The man I worked for in the fish markets. Tony Basile." At his start of recognition, I remembered when they'd met. "Ah, the man in the cross-country motorcycle race who took a tumble in the river with you on the last lap."

"That idiot? You walked out with that idiot?" It seemed I'd only thrown fuel on the fire of his fury. "He cut me off in the race and I'd have damn near killed him if I hadn't swerved and gone into the river instead. Damn near lost my motorcycle, too. Now I want to kill him more than ever for even thinking he had a chance with you, lass. My God…"

My temper flared up. "Tony was my employer and my friend, William. Yes, he wanted to be more. I was lonely and I enjoyed his company and while you were busy ignoring me all over Fremantle, he asked me to marry him."

"But I…but you…I wanted you to be my wife. What did you say to him?" William demanded.

I yanked my arm from his grasp. "You never asked me. Not once. You spoke of what you wanted on the ship, but you never asked me."

The anguish in his eyes broke my heart. "But you didn't understand. You didn't speak English. How could I have asked you to marry me when you didn't know what I was asking you to do? I consider myself an honourable man. I couldn't coerce you into a marriage you might not want." He swallowed. "Maria, what did you tell him? When he asked you, what was your answer?"

"I didn't answer him. I bade him good night and that's all. The following day, I boarded the *Islander* in Fremantle and you know the rest."

His eyebrows scrunched together as his face grew as thunderous as the sky last week. "I'm beginning to think there's a lot I don't know, and I aim to find out. Now you're my wife, there should be no secrets between us and —"

A grinning Chinese man burst through the door and out onto the veranda. "Tuan! The *Islander* brought Frankenstein's monster!" He triumphantly held up a film reel. "This isn't even in Singapore yet. Can we show this at tonight's cinema?"

William made a vague, affirmative reply that made the man grin more widely than ever.

"Will you come to the cinema to watch the scary monster movie, Mem?" the man asked politely. "You are Tuan's sister, yes?"

William coughed. "This is my wife, Mrs McGregor. My sister, Mrs Whyte, is still in Scotland, as far as I know, though she keeps writing and telling me how much she'd like to visit."

His sister? The woman he'd talked about on the ship? The true owner of my precious tortoiseshell comb.

William nudged me and I realised the Chinese man was looking at me expectantly. Awkwardly, I apologised and asked him to repeat his question.

"No question, Mem. I only said I was honoured to meet you and I hope you enjoy your stay on Christmas Island."

"A pleasure, Mr – " I realised that neither he nor William had told me the man's name.

He flashed another grin. "Ong, Mem. If your husband had warned us of your arrival, we'd have planned a banquet in your honour."

I managed an answering smile. "A pleasure, Mr Ong."

A glance at William's scowl stopped me from saying more as he seized my arm and hustled me back down the stairs.

<h1 style="text-align:center">Five</h1>

William muttered under his breath most of the way up the road, and I caught phrases like, "Nosy Chinese bastard," and other less than complimentary terms which seemed directed at the innocuous Mr Ong. It wasn't until we were halfway back to the house, with no one within earshot, that William finally released my arm.

"William, please stop cursing that man and his ancestry, and tell me what the problem is.

I'm beginning to see why they call you Grumpy. I'm surprised they don't call you anything worse."

He made as if to grab my arm again, but I stepped back, out of reach.

"I crossed the ocean for the William McGregor who risked his own life to rescue me from a raft, a kind man who did his utmost to protect a girl he knew nothing about. One who talked and laughed and promised to take care of me. One who loved me, or said he did. Not some hard, grumpy man who never smiles and refuses to explain his rude behaviour." I stood my ground and lifted my chin, as I had the first time he'd argued with me on the *Trevessa*. This time, I wouldn't back down.

If anything, William's scowl deepened. His breath hissed out. "I didn't like the way he looked at you." My disbelief must have been written clearly across my face, for he continued, "He was staring at your legs. You're…wait, you're not even wearing stockings? Lass, I thought you said you knew what you were doing!"

He expected me to wear stockings in this heat? They'd be soaked with sweat within moments. Even in summer in Fremantle I'd gone without. "Ladies don't wear stockings when it's this hot," I mumbled, but he didn't seem to hear me.

"He looked at you like he wanted to buy you, and he was guessing your price. First Basile, now Ong…and I remember how the men on the *Trevessa* looked at you, too. I mean to protect you, Maria, just like I promised." His expression softened.

I sighed. Ocean preserve me from jealous husbands. And stockings. "So the problem is that you're jealous of other men even looking at me with admiration? Mr Ong was friendly, no more. William, I do know the difference. If you object to men looking at me, then I suggest you learn to ignore it. All men look at me and most of them admire my appearance." A sudden thought struck me. "Don't you find me attractive? Am I ugly to your eyes?"

"God, no!" When he grabbed my shoulders, I didn't resist. He stared deep into my eyes. "I know you're the most beautiful woman I've ever seen, far too beautiful to be my wife. And when others see it and want to take you away from me…"

I stretched up and lightly kissed his lips. "They'll find themselves in very deep trouble, because there's only one man I crossed the Indian Ocean for, and I want no other. I'll fight for you as fiercely as I've seen you fight for me, William. Now, when were you going to tell me about your sister's visit?"

His gaze dropped to his shoes. "I'd completely forgotten, to be honest. All the excitement at finding you again and then the cyclone… James' father died recently and his mother moved in with them to help Sarah with the children. But now the children are at school for the term, Sarah wants to leave Morag to take care of James so she can make good on her promise to visit me. I've written so many letters, telling her about you and the

Trevessa and all the strange things here on Christmas Island, she's been saying for years that she'd take ship across the world. I didn't believe her at first, but she won't let go of the idea. I haven't given her a date yet, but if I know her, she won't be put off for much longer. Before I know it, she'll be on her way to Singapore. The first news we'll have of her arrival in Singapore will probably come on the *Islander*…with her aboard."

I managed to smile, though I felt more nervous than I had any reason to be. "Then we should get going on this island tour you've promised me. Your sister will surely want me to show her around the island and if we delay much longer, she'll arrive before I even know the most picturesque spots."

William's smiled seemed more genuine than mine and it oozed relief, too. "Very well. Shall we?" He held out his arm and I took it for the climb back up to his bungalow at Rocky Point.

Six

When we reached the house, William said, "I should go change. You don't happen to have a pair of riding pants, do you?" He eyed my skirt.

Riding pants? I tried not to laugh. "Of course not. The only riding I intended to do here is best without pants."

To my delight, William reddened. "I meant on a motorcycle," he mumbled.

It was my turn to blush. "No. Merry and I didn't own a horse, and though I rode my bicycle to work, I did so in a skirt. Though if I'd gotten around to buying a motorcycle like I wanted to, I might have bought appropriate clothing. Perhaps…perhaps I could wear some of yours?"

William choked. I took his discomfiture as a *no*.

"Where can I buy my own here, then?"

He coughed and cleared his throat several times before replying, "You can't. I'll have to take you to Singapore to buy clothes. When the *Islander* returns, I will. Until then…I suppose a skirt will have to do."

"Better than naked," I ventured, though I didn't mean a word of it. Just as long as he didn't try and insist I wear stockings again.

"Yes. Absolutely, a million times yes," he said fervently.

I followed him into the house, wondering why he felt the need to change. His present pants were perfectly practical for cycling – was motorcycling so different? I settled on the bed while he dropped his trousers. Sadly, his drawers stayed on, as he pulled on a pair that fitted more tightly than the ones he'd just shed. In fact, it didn't look like fabric at all. I stretched a hand out to touch his leg. More like… "Leather?" I asked, stroking the stuff as it warmed with his body heat.

"Yes," he said shortly, pulling his boots on again. He led the way back outside, where I could hear the putter of a motor. The sound stopped before I reached the veranda, but I slowed my approach all the same, for now I could hear men's voices speaking Chinese.

William charged down the steps, congratulating the men. I managed a more decorous descent, keeping one hand on the railing until I reached the ground.

"What do you think?" William asked, waving at his motorcycle. The men moved aside so I could see it.

The wire shelf I'd refused yesterday now sported a bench seat of sorts. It looked like a plank wrapped in a piece of worn leather, then nailed in place behind the existing seat so that a passenger could sit behind the rider. The thickness of the plank made the springs no longer an issue – the only thing between my legs would be William. Hoping to hide my smile at that thought, I glanced down. A pair of additional footrests had been added to the frame, too.

When I raised my eyes, it seemed everyone was still waiting for my reaction. I tried to channel a little of Merry's dignity and composure to stop myself from thinking about sex, for surely it would show in my expression. "I think it's quite an improvement. Thank you."

This seemed sufficient, as William repeated my words in Chinese and the other men grinned.

William lifted me in his arms and carried me to the Triumph, setting me sideways on the seat so my legs hung off one side and threatened to unbalance the motorcycle.

William was quick to take the driver's seat in front of me, grabbing a pair of goggles off the handlebars and shoving them down over his eyes.

"Hold on, lass!" he shouted, stomping down on the kickstart lever.

The engine coughed irritably.

He stomped twice more before the motor stopped expectorating and cleared its throat. It settled into a steady ticking, which seemed to satisfy William, so he shoved the kickstand, dropping me and the rear tyre with a jarring bump before the tyres found traction in the mud and we started to move downhill. I wrapped one arm around William, for sitting side-on to him made anything else too difficult, and clutched at my hat in my other hand as each bump and rut in the road seemed set on prying it loose from my head, four hatpins or no.

We lurched through a pothole and I rose almost a foot off the seat before smacking back down again. "Stop!" I shouted at William.

No way in water was I riding a motorcycle like this. I'd rather walk.

He slowed and I jumped off before he halted. William jerked his goggles off his face. "It's all right, lass," he soothed, patting the air with his hands as he approached. "There's nothing to be afraid of. I won't let you fall off as long as you hold on to me. I won't go fast, I'll take it easy and – "

"William, having me sitting sideways on that thing throws it off balance. The…I'm not sure of the word for it, but the weight distribution is wrong. As it is, we'd have a smoother ride with me driving and you sitting on the back – and I don't know what I'm doing."

He looked shocked. "But…your skirt…and your modesty…and…you mean you're not scared?"

I burst out laughing. "I'm scared of having my teeth rattled out of my head if we keep going as we have, but that's about it. I'll wrap my skirt around my legs and try not to show anyone my drawers. I managed it on a bicycle every day in Fremantle. I'm sure there are far fewer people here." I leaned forward so that my nose almost touched his. "Get back on the Triumph. I'll mount up behind you and hold on. This is my first ride on a motorcycle, something I've wanted for a very long time. Make it one to remember, William." I winked.

Still he hesitated. "You'll tell me if you do feel frightened, won't you? Or if I'm going too fast for you?"

Too fast? For a moment, I wished I could show him how fast I could be…in the storm swell of a cyclone, racing dolphins through the waves to see who could fly the farthest. But no, William could never know what I was.

"Sure," I said instead. "Can we go now?" I couldn't keep the eagerness out of my voice.

Seven

Speed was the last thing he needed to worry about as we started our ascent to the top of the cliffs. William adjusted the levers on his handlebars and I peered over his shoulder, trying to work out what he was doing.

William turned his head slightly and I saw the corner of his mouth lift in a smile. He tapped the lever on the left and shouted, 'I use this one to retard the spark, because we're slowing to go up a hill."

I nodded and my chin bumped his shoulder.

"This one controls the air and this one's the throttle, to make it go faster," William continued, tapping each of the right hand levers in turn. "But don't worry, we won't be going any faster for a bit. Slow and steady up to the plateau."

"Then can we go faster? A plateau is flat, yes?"

"If that's what you want, lass."

I hugged him tighter. Not because I was afraid and needed the reassurance, but because I was happy and wanted to thank him for doing this for me. This was the man I'd crossed the ocean for – the only one who'd give me my heart's desire.

True to his word, when we crested the rise, William shifted the levers again and we accelerated. "This is where they first started mining for phosphate, but these bits were mined out before I arrived. The rich deposits down near South Point are what the company's mining now." He pointed off to the left. "Over that way's Margaret Knoll. There's a huge colony of fruit bats, the ones that fly around the veranda at night, living in the trees around there."

Bats? I'd seen them when I'd prowled around the island, but aside from the one that fell in my soup last night, I didn't find them particularly interesting.

"Here's where we join the railway line, and we'll follow that all the way to South Point." The track curved around some trees and we shot out into a clearing bisected by a set of train tracks. Fortunately, there was no train in sight. I stared at the buildings that edged the tracks, wondering if it was my imagination, or whether they were as deserted as they seemed. After all, they looked like copies of the kampung houses along Flying Fish Cove, only newer and not damaged in a landslide. I caught movement out of the corner of my eye, but when I looked more closely at the doorway, all I saw was a robber crab, backing slowly into the darkness.

"Who lives here?" I asked, nodding toward the houses.

"No one. It's just one of the construction camps the coolies used while they were building the rail line."

I wondered if I was missing something. "So it's vacant? And there's enough space for everyone who lost their houses in the landslide yesterday? Or are they staying with your friend Jackson indefinitely and he's moving up here?"

William stiffened and I debated whether I should have kept my mouth shut. This wasn't a particularly practical place when it came to politics between the different groups of people, but I'd seen the same sort of bigotry in Fremantle, too. What would humans say if they knew my people claimed fatherhood from all of the races of humans around the Indian Ocean, yet lived together in harmony, regardless of the colour of our skin, tails and hair? Not that I'd seen humans with skin the colour of my turquoise tail, or the deep-water blue of my mother's and my daughter's tails. A wave of longing swept over me at the thought of my daughter, stolen from me even before I was exiled.

No, I told myself. Thinking about her would only bring on the agony of loss that had paralysed me on the raft when William first met me. She was well-cared for by my people and better off without a mother who had no place among the people of the ocean's gift, which I never would, as long as I refused to bow down to the Indian Ocean Elder Council's crushing authority. So they might live in harmony…but not with me. Perhaps I shouldn't have told that pack of domineering old women what I'd thought of them and their so-called authority.

I allowed myself a moment to wish things had been different. That Giuseppe had lived; that I'd skimmed happily through the waves all the way home to the shallows at Cocos, then given birth to our daughter and taken my place as Mother's heir and eventual successor to her position on the Elder Council. I'd have been able to watch my daughter grow from a giggling baby into a child who could shift from tail to legs and back again, learning to sing her siren's song to enslave every creature in the ocean. She'd have tamed her first shark by now, surely. Perhaps even now Mother was grooming her to be her heir instead of me. The poor child – she'd be subject to lessons and lectures from the cold Elder Sephira, the same taskmistress I'd been forced to call Mother as I obeyed her orders to the letter until I'd lost Giuseppe. If it weren't for William, my heart might still be broken. And then I'd almost lost him in yet another shipwreck…

I loosened my grip as William slowed down.

"Is everything all right? How are you holding up?" He glanced over his shoulder at me.

Figuring I must have given some indication of my inner turmoil, I deliberately turned my mind to more pleasant things and kissed his cheek. "Absolutely fine. Don't stop on my account. But if there's a train coming…does the train take the phosphate all the way into the port where the ships are loaded?"

William laughed. "It does for the most part, but it's been very slow bringing the ore cars down the incline. We had this brilliant idea to build a chute from Drumsite down to the shunting yard above the cove and it's currently under construction. When it's finished next year, the trains can dump their load at Drumsite and the phosphate will go sliding down the cliff on a giant slippery-dip to the bottom, like a child at a fair."

"Won't it get stuck?" I blurted out, thinking of the children back in Fremantle who wet themselves in excitement partway down their slide and then needed a push to make it the rest of the way. "I mean, you're mining mud from the back ends of birds in a tropical climate. I imagine it's very wet. Not to mention the amount of rain you get here. How often will it clog up? And what will you do to unblock it?"

"Our calculations show it'll be just fine. Don't worry, lass. We engineers always know what we're doing, and I've been doing this job for a long time."

I shrugged. If he was wrong about his glorified plumbing pipe, it wouldn't be my problem. After all, what did a mermaid know about these things? Plumbing wasn't really necessary under water. You just waved your tail a bit and it…well, went away. Or you did.

We passed a second deserted work camp, but William didn't slow down. Instead, he veered away from the railway track into the jungle, with vegetation close enough to touch as we wove between the trees on a track barely wide enough for the motorcycle. We rounded a bend and the trees just ended. All I could see were stone pinnacles and mud, which a gang of the Chinese and Malay men were shovelling away from the rock. It looked like a horrible job.

They ducked their heads and touched their foreheads in what I assumed was a sign of respect as we passed, but William didn't acknowledge the gesture. I nodded a little, but I'm not sure if they saw or even cared, as they went back to shovelling straight away.

"They have a quota to fill each day and they get bonuses if they do more than their share," William explained after a while. "It doesn't pay to stop to chat, not when the difference could mean an extra night in the opium den or the brothel…or the money to bring a wife over and not have to live in the single men's quarters."

Ah, this I certainly understood. The same sort of determination drove the Fremantle fishermen – a few hours out in that winter storm catching a bumper load of snapper had won Tony the money for his motorcycle. And granted me a decent chunk of the funds I'd set aside to search for William. Money I could now spend on a motorcycle, so I could ride beside William, if he'd teach me how.

"William, will you show me how to drive your Triumph?" I asked.

He didn't say anything for a long moment, while I wondered if he'd heard me or if I needed to repeat my words.

Finally, he said, "Are you sure you want to, lass? It's not usually something women do and it can be dangerous. I wouldn't want you to get hurt."

"More dangerous than swimming with sharks? Or riding on the back of yours while you're driving?"

"No. No, not really." I felt him sigh. "Sure, lass. Maybe on the way home from South Point. But first, I need to check the pumps. Starting with this one, the infernal engine at Ross Hill." He circled the Triumph and halted outside a brick building nestled in the middle of a network of pipes. "I swear the man who designed the hot bulb engine must have sold his soul to the devil and gotten a poor bargain in return. It may run on any old fuel, but it guzzles it down faster than any other engine I've ever worked with. And if it runs out of fuel…starting it up again is a devil of a job."

He eyed the building, not appearing particularly eager to head inside.

"Do you need my help?" I ventured.

William laughed. "No, lass, the pump house is no place for a lady. And if I have to heat the bulbs up to start the engine again, even if they use paraffin and not coal, I don't want you fainting on me like you did when you saw the ship's boilers on the *Trevessa*."

I frowned, trying to remember what he meant. My frown deepened as I realised his memory clashed with mine. "I didn't faint. I merely believed the ship was on fire. The last time I saw a ship on fire, many people died and the ship sank. I may not be as naïve now as I was then, but as I recall, even the men who set the *Emden* on fire seemed shocked by the damage they'd caused. And that was war." I didn't mention that the same battle had killed my sister, enraging an eight-year-old girl who took a terrible revenge, letting the ship burn without cease as I diverted the waves that might have extinguished them.

My expression must have spoken for me, though, as William chose to pull me into his arms for a few minutes, just as he had outside the *Trevessa*'s engine room. Then I'd feared that the humans had a similar fate in store for me, because they'd known what I did to their comrades. Now…I knew better.

"Stay close to the buildings and don't wander far. There are coolies working in the plantations here and some of the men have never seen a woman as beautiful as you before. I'll be as quick as I can." William disappeared into the building.

Feeling sticky with the humidity and wishing for a swim, I leaned back along the body of his Triumph, starting up at the wispy clouds. Perhaps I could persuade William to detour to the Grotto on the way back.

Eight

"I thought I said not to wander far."

I stopped skimming my toes through the shallow water and turned to face William. "I didn't. I realised the pipes went somewhere and the stream looked so inviting, I couldn't resist. It was only a few steps to the stream and the locals didn't bother me." I waved at the collection of crabs keeping their distance on the other side of a rotting log. They understood my command to stay away from me and my shoes, though William wouldn't. Good thing, too. We'd been separated for long enough. "Are we going to ride some more?"

He stared at me in wonderment, a wry smile on his face. "All that time when you couldn't talk, I wondered what you'd say if you could. And now, every time you open your mouth, you surprise me. Is there anything at all that you fear?"

I slipped my shoes on and rose. "Losing those I love." I'd lost too many of them already. And I wouldn't lose William again.

William bowed his head, all traces of humour gone. "I understand. You won't lose me, lass. Not as long as I live. And I'll never let go of you, I swear."

I wanted to believe him, but the ocean was more powerful than us both. And who knew what the future held? Not to mention his threat to return me to Fremantle if I wasn't the perfect wife. I glanced down at my mud-spattered legs. It would've been worse with stockings. At least I could splash water on my legs to wash away the mud.

"Would you like to see one of the best views on the island? The damn engine was running in reverse, so I need to check the water levels." William pointed at the tank on top of the cliff, high above us. "You managed the ladders on the ship like you were born on the water. That one shouldn't be any trouble for you."

"You'd like me to do your job for you?"

"No, lass. Being my wife makes you a lady of leisure. I'll be right behind you. You're just coming to enjoy the view and I'll explain what you're seeing, if you like."

I nodded and headed for the cliff. Scaling the ladder was far simpler than scaling the cliff above the Grotto and the view was everything William had promised. I could see the ocean, closer than I'd expected it to be, and plenty of frigatebirds soaring on the thermals down to the water to catch their morning meal.

"Did you see South Point?"

I turned at the sound of William's voice, but

his warm arm around my waist pulled me in a different direction entirely. I sighted along his outstretched arm as he pointed at the community perched on the southern cliffs, gaps in the trees signifying the presence of quarries and train lines, and the plume of smoke that marked one of the locomotives headed back to Flying Fish Cove.

"Those are the coolie lines…the gantry…and the manager's bungalow. He's an engineer, like me, and he's offered me all sorts of things to get me to switch with him – he wants me to manage South Point while he manages the port, water and power supply. Up until now, I've refused, but if you wanted to, I'd do it. More privacy, less danger of landslides, more authority, more responsibility…and there'd be fewer people at South Point, so I wouldn't worry about you so much."

His arm had grown uncomfortably tight around my waist, so I shifted out of his grasp. "Isolation doesn't suit me. I saw enough of that to last a lifetime on my tiny raft. Besides, I don't think this place will be isolated long. Mining has moved so close to this spot it would be silly not to move all the displaced miners here or the inland work camps. As you say, less risk of landslides. Why haven't they already moved?"

William patted the tank. "Water. Until we get this old engine replaced, we won't have a reliable water supply for South Point. As it is, they run out some days and have to send someone down here to fill a water barrel."

I surveyed the distance between us and the tiny houses on the cliff. "That's a long way for water. How does it travel so far?"

"There's another pumping station at South Point with a newer engine, but it can only pump water from this top tank. The Ross Hill pump here takes water from the stream, fills the bottom tank, then pumps it up to the top one. That's why we have plantations here — it's where the water is. Look — that's where we grow all our coffee, rubber and hemp for rope." William sighed. "Before the storm, a replacement for this pump was next on my list of equipment. Now, it looks like we'll have to replace the pier and all the houses, too. Not to mention the sheds, gantries, roads and rail in the cove. I'll be dealing with this old devil for the next decade at least."

"Can't you say the pump got damaged in the storm? It looks like you'd save a fair bit of money by simply not replacing what the landslide destroyed. If you have a new pump, the houses here would be usable, right?" I ventured.

"Oh, only the South Point settlement uses water from Ross Hill. The work camps take their drinking water from Grant's Well, where the windmill was a ways back."

"So you have two functional camps for the men who are staying with Mr Jackson, an excuse to develop your South Point settlement further and replace the pump that seems to be the bane of your existence…what more could you ask for?"

William still didn't smile. "I'd need the company manager to agree. Christmas Island Phosphate Company. That's not Jackson, that's Murray and he's not here. He might even come for an inspection – his letters mention it every year, though I've never seen him set foot on the island."

"It's worth a shot, isn't it, William?"

He nodded, too lost in thought to say much else. He led the way down the ladder to the Triumph.

"Are we headed back now? Is it time for my riding lesson?" I asked eagerly.

He managed a faint smile. "First I need to check the pumping station at South Point and speak to the manager there, fill up the fuel tank, and then I'll try to show you how to ride this contraption."

Nine

South Point didn't look much different from ground level – just a lot bigger. Especially the gantry that towered over the houses. The lonely manager, who'd mumbled his name so unintelligibly that I hadn't managed to catch it, had invited us to tea in his bungalow, but I took one look at William's rigid stance and politely declined, to William's evident relief. Did he think tea and cake was a ritual I couldn't manage?

He was probably right, I reluctantly admitted to myself. If it was anything like the tea William drank, I'd struggle to be polite enough not to spit it out, and I was eager for my riding lesson. I almost skipped back to the pump house, where he'd left the Triumph.

He explained the control levers again as I bounced eagerly in my seat. Spark, air, fuel. Brake to slow it down. Slow right down and lean in to the corner to turn, just like riding a bicycle. And then William lifted his leg over the passenger seat and settled in behind me, firmly wrapping his arms across my belly. A belly that was suddenly full of rabid butterflies.

William leaned forward, so that my back rested against a wall of warm, hard muscle. "Are you ready, lass?"

I didn't hesitate. "Yes," I breathed.

He gave a little jump and jarred the Triumph as he slammed his foot down on the kickstart lever. The engine caught on the first time. "Now adjust everything until the engine sounds just right – like it did on the ride up here."

I closed my eyes, hearing the steady beat of the sparks, feeling the bass thrumming through my thighs and smelling the acrid fumes of fuel burning. "Easy does it," I murmured and pushed off with my foot. We accelerated easily down the gentle slope, but the muddy track was rapidly coming to an end.

"Slow down and lean into the turn, lass."

I gritted my teeth and did just that, easing off on the throttle so that I barely even needed the brake. I rounded the curve clumsily, needing to touch the ground with my feet to steady us, but I made it. My hand shook a little as I opened up the throttle again for the straight stretch along the railway line. I whooped as the wind blew my hair back, knowing we were moving faster than I could swim. It was like flying. And with the hot, vibrating engine between my legs, incredibly sensual, too. What would William say if I told him that it wasn't the other men on the island he needed to be jealous of…but his own motorcycle?

I laughed aloud.

"Are you enjoying yourself, lass?"

"Yes, oh yes!" I grinned. "You just wait until we're alone with no clothes on so I can thank you properly for this." Oh, all the things I'd longed to do to him…I wanted to get that book out of my trunk, that *Kama Sutra* one, so I could turn some of my longing fantasies into wonderful reality.

"Okay, we're going up a hill now, so you'll need to retard the – " William slid forward, reaching past me to adjust the levers. His thighs were firm alongside mine, sandwiching me neatly between his legs. He didn't shift back again, keeping one hand lightly on the handlebars while the other circled my waist. I grew increasingly aware of the warm leather bulging behind my backside and I felt an escalating heat in my nether regions, the desire building to abandon the motorcycle and yield to him completely. Overpowering my mind and my other senses…

I saw the track that led to the Grotto and veered right, braking carefully. Not carefully enough – William's momentum pushed us closer together so all I could think about was riding him and not the motorcycle.

The Triumph crunched to a halt on the leaf litter and the engine shuddered into silence. I spun in my seat so I faced him. William eased off the passenger seat just as I slid onto it. Disappointment sent a faint twinge through me. He engaged the stand, jolting me back to reality.

"Are you all right? Have you had enough driving for one day?" he asked. "I can drive us home if you want."

I wanted…sex more than I craved air. Wanted it? No, needed it. I yanked off my drawers and plucked at the hem on my skirt. "I want you, William. Here, now."

Naked desire danced in his eyes, even if his pants hadn't given him away. I ached even as I looked at him. I pulled off my dress and threw it over the handlebars.

William's eyes widened.

I couldn't summon the self-control to get off the Triumph. Instead, I sat on the edge of the passenger seat and lay back, so my head rested on the fuel tank. For a moment, I let my legs dangle off the back as I struggled to remove my brassiere. I hung that from the handlebars, too, on top of my drawers.

The hunger in William's eyes matched the burn I felt deep inside. He strode forward so he was close enough to reach out and touch me, but he didn't.

I lifted my legs into the air and crossed my ankles behind his neck. "I need to feel you inside me. Please, William. Take me."

This time he didn't hesitate. His belt clinked and my breath caught in my throat with eager anticipation. He plunged in deep, unleashing a groan that drowned out whatever noise I made at the bliss of being finally filled with the heat he'd tantalised me with during the ride.

I couldn't think beyond the feel of him, all I

wanted was more and harder and yes, oh yes, don't stop. Even as I shrieked my joy when he sent shockwaves of pleasure through me, I was begging him for more. And by water, he gave it to me. The pounding surf was nothing to our frenzied lovemaking. I wanted to continue forever, to be joined to him in ecstasy for as long as I drew breath. Moaning, panting breath…

I let out a wail of anguish as he pulled out of me, leaving me bereft. Firm hands pried my legs apart from their lock around his neck.

Panting, he said, "Are you…trying to…kill me with loving, lass? I…hope I didn't hurt you. You just looked at me like that and you looked like that and you begged me…and I seem to have lost control of my mind. All I wanted was you."

My insides flooded with heat, eager for more.

What was wrong with me? I'd been just as out of my mind with rampant lust. Well-placed rampant lust, yes, for I wanted William as much as I loved life, but this felt like madness. Was this what my songs engendered in men? Then how had it affected me – when I hadn't sung at all?

I became aware of my uncomfortable headrest and sat up. What crazed person would want to have sex on a motorcycle? There was scarcely room for it. And where were we?

I glanced around, noticing the familiar clearing ending in rocks. The Grotto.

"We should go for a swim to cool off a little," I suggested, trying to ignore the ache between my thighs that didn't want to cool anything off. One glance at William and I wanted to throw myself at him on the forest floor, to make love all over again. Instead, I forced myself to turn my back and walk toward the cave. A quick descent sent my feet splashing into the shallow water. I glanced up to see William on the cliff above, watching me as he undressed. Heat burned inside me. "Come join me," I begged him – the words left my mouth before I'd thought to speak. "Please, William. I need you."

And I did.

He splashed down behind me, sending a wave of water up my legs as he strode through the pool. William pressed against my back, pulling me hard against him, so I could feel that I wasn't the only one who needed to quench a raging urge. His body shouldn't be capable of recovering so fast – surely he needed to recharge somewhat? – but I could feel the evidence to the contrary hard against my back.

"Maria…do you think – "

I didn't think. I took a step backwards, pinning him to the cave wall, then leaned over and grabbed my ankles. "Oh, please," I begged.

William didn't leave me wanting.

Ten

Some time later, thoroughly worn out, William mumbled something about needing to return home for lunch.

Lunch. Food. To fuel the stamina we needed to join again just as powerfully. I clambered up the cliff to the clearing and headed for the Triumph.

The sound of William clearing his throat made me look up.

"Lass, you need to put your clothes back on. Can't ride back to Settlement naked."

I glanced down, bemused, to find that I sat astride the warm leather with not even my drawers on.

Lusty mermaids don't need clothes, I thought, but the respectable Mrs McGregor did, or she'd be sent back to Fremantle in disgrace. I sighed and dressed. I found myself yawning and struggling to keep my eyes open by the time we arrived at William's bungalow, and barely able to voice more than a feeble protest as he hoisted me in his arms.

Darkness enveloped us as he moved from the steps to the veranda and the cool interior of the house. I felt something cool and soft beneath me. I barely had time to register that William had taken me to bed before I surrendered to oblivion.

Eleven

Something cold and wet touched my forehead. Not an unusual occurrence when you're used to sleeping underwater, but certainly jarring when I realised I was still in William's bed. No, our bed.

"William?" I croaked.

"I sent to the kitchen for some tea, but I'm not sure if you should drink it. It has a foreign smell to it," a distinctly feminine voice said.

Her accent marked her as Scottish, like William and Jackson. "I'll send it back and insist on the proper stuff. With milk."

I inhaled experimentally and caught the faint whiff of jasmine. My tea. Thanking Cook silently for remembering, I sat up, scanning the darkened room for the source of the smell. When I spotted the saucer, I seized the cup and downed the lukewarm contents in two gulps.

"No, it's fine," I said. "Drinking tea without milk is a habit I picked up in Australia."

"So that's where Mr McGregor's been hiding you," she replied. "When my husband told me Mr McGregor had a wife and she was here on the island, you could have knocked me down with a feather. I'd have sworn he was a bachelor for life, but I caught him on his way up to the wireless station to invite him to dinner and he said it would depend on his wife's health, as he couldn't accept the invitation without you. He said you were unwell and I promised I'd come to check on you. I was a nurse in the Great War, you see, not to mention raising two children here. Jean's at school in Scotland now, but Alan's not to go yet. Good thing, too, or I wouldn't have anyone to translate what our houseguests are saying. I know the poor coolies have lost their houses in the landslide, but our home is hardly the place for them. Mr McGregor said he was radioing for what was needed to give these men a new roof over their heads, so I shooed him away and promised to take care of you. The heat does for all of us when we first arrive. Not like England or Scotland."

I managed a smile. "I wouldn't know. The heat in Australia takes some getting used to, too."

Her eyes narrowed. "So it's not the heat making you feel unwell? Perhaps it's the mother's malady and you'll soon be giving Mr McGregor a son?" She eyed my midsection as if she thought my imagined pregnancy should be so advanced as to be obvious.

"No, I'm not carrying a child yet. At least,

not that I know of. Too early to say, I imagine. William and I…never had a wedding night and last night was our first night together…" I drifted off, wondering whether I should say that we'd gotten very little sleep because we'd tried to squeeze seven years' worth of sex into one night. Not to mention today's marathon effort.

She patted my shoulder sympathetically. "Ah, your first time can come as a bit of a shock. But men have needs. It's either you or his mistress and the women at the White House…well, what would you prefer?" I didn't like her knowing smile. William had a mistress? "You're young and strong — you'll grow accustomed to his night-time attentions. After all, it's over within a few minutes."

A few minutes? I almost choked. What sort of clumsy lover was her husband? Or did she mean William? Had she slept with William? Was this woman William's mistress? My fury ignited, but I tried to bite it back. "I was widowed before I met William, so it was hardly my first time. And I am accustomed to…more than a few minutes." There. Chew on that, strange snippy woman.

She regarded me shrewdly. "When did you meet Mr McGregor?"

"On the *Trevessa*, when he was on his way here."

Her eyes widened. "So how did he come to arrive without you, if you were travelling together on the same ship?"

Was this a test, or did she truly not know that the *Trevessa* sank? I wondered. "The ship left Fremantle, but never made its next port. William and I were separated the night the *Trevessa* sank – I in one lifeboat and he in another. His lifeboat travelled to Mauritius, I understand. A miraculous journey. My boat was luckier – we were picked up by a search vessel, the *Trevean*, after only two days drifting at sea. Her captain brought me to Fremantle in Western Australia, where I've been living with my aunt."

Wide awake now, there was no way I

wanted to sleep for longer and with William gone, I had no need to linger in bed, either. "Please excuse me, Mrs…I don't believe you've told me your name." I could guess, though.

"Jackson. Anne Jackson. My husband is the acting island manager."

My first guess had been correct. I only hoped I was wrong about William sleeping with his boss's wife.

"Well, excuse me, please, Mrs Jackson, but I need to freshen up. If you give me a few minutes, I might be able to invite you to tea, unless William's cook chases me out of the kitchen again."

Mrs Jackson nodded curtly and retreated to the hallway outside. "You will tell me if you need my assistance, won't you? I told Mr McGregor I'd take care of you, you see, and I'd feel responsible if…"

As she spoke, I changed into a fresh dress and brushed my hair. I'd pinned it so firmly that only a few wisps had escaped, so unpinning it now left me with a mane of curls – quite unusual for me. Anne wore a hat, but I slipped on a hairband instead and left my hair otherwise unrestrained.

I stepped into the passage beside her. "Am I presentable for my first Christmas Island afternoon tea, Mrs Jackson?"

She pressed her lips together as she looked me up and down. "Call me Anne, please," she said grudgingly. But she didn't say a word about my appearance. Did that mean it was acceptable or not?

I swallowed and inclined my head. "Maria," I managed to say.

Twelve

Anne led the way through my house as if she was the mistress here and not me. I owned that she was more familiar with the place than I surely was, but I wondered why. Had she and Jackson come visiting often, or just her? Had her husband's lack of skill in the bedroom driven her into William's lonely arms? She had to be ten years older than me, I estimated, but she was the first European woman I'd seen here. Perhaps the only one on the island, given my origins. I wondered if the faint twinge I felt inside was jealousy.

No and no, I told myself. William's energetic lovemaking spoke of long abstinence. He couldn't have spent even a few minutes with this woman. Not to mention the problems it would cause with her husband and his superior. You couldn't keep a secret like that in a community this small. Especially with servants in the house and on watch outside. Yet I'd managed to slip into William's bedroom at night, unseen. Jackson's wife could have done the same…and if it only took a few minutes that she didn't enjoy, perhaps she'd been quiet enough for no one to hear or notice a thing…my heart cried out in horror.

Instead of the kitchen, I followed Anne into the dining room.

"I hope you don't mind," she said, "but I took the liberty of ordering afternoon tea."

I pressed my lips together to silence my angry reply. Of course I minded. She'd ordered people around in my house. She wouldn't take any more liberties in my and William's house, I swore. And if she ever thought of opening her legs for William again…

"I had my cook send some cakes and sandwiches over, as yours hasn't had much reason to learn to make them, what with the men only having lunch and all," she continued and shot a doubtful glance at me. "I take it your cook can prepare tea and your girl can serve it?"

I met Cook's eyes as I entered the room. Her gaze slid to the perfect tea and coffee service on the sideboard, but the disgruntled set of her mouth told me she'd heard Anne's disdain. Well, we were both in accord on that one. Neither of us liked the annoying Mrs Jackson. Time to put her in her place.

"Better than I can, I suspect," I replied firmly. "Thank you."

The faintest smile touched Cook's lips, but she turned away before I could be certain.

Anne didn't seem to have noticed my words

at all, as she took a seat at the table and I followed suit. Amah appeared from nowhere and she and Cook busied themselves with crockery and the tea service until both Anne and I had steaming cups before us. Cook set a selection of dainty cakes on the table between us – far more than two people could eat – and ushered Amah out of the room.

I wanted to thank them, or offer them a seat at the table to share the cakes Anne had brought, but as I opened my mouth, Cook shook her head slightly, as if warning me not to say anything.

More rules I didn't understand. Frustrated, I reached for the nearest cake, a golden brown rectangle with tiny pinpricks along the top, and bit deeply into it. The cake disintegrated in my mouth, as if the sweet, gritty stuff it was made from dissolved the moment it grew damp. It was lucky to have survived this long in the humidity.

"So you like Scottish shortbread?" Anne asked, selecting a small tart with a delicate pair of tongs that I hadn't seen.

I swallowed quickly. "I think I might. It's not something I've seen much of in Australia." I set the remains down on my plate.

"Or afternoon tea, either," Anne said sharply. "You don't know much about high society life, do you? You're supposed to start with the savoury items first."

My heart sank, but anger rose in its place. "No. Australia's a practical place. Sitting around eating cakes all afternoon according to some sort of hierarchy isn't something I usually have time for. One cake, perhaps, and a cup of tea, then back to work. We didn't have servants to wait on us hand and foot as if we were invalids." I reached for the sweetest-looking cake I could find – something covered in chocolate – and popped the entire thing in my mouth.

Anne's composure didn't change. "Or in Scotland, which is why I enjoy my time here so much. I'm a terrible cook, so I think it's a relief for Jackson not to have to eat the dubious results of my attempts at cooking." Despite her calm exterior, I sensed a turbulence inside her that matched mine. Was this what William had liked in her, enough to take her as his mistress? Could I ever be enough to satisfy him so he'd never turn to her again?

I managed to swallow the chocolate pastry, resolving to eat it in at least two bites next time, and voiced the thought on the tip of my tongue. "I'm not what you expected of William's wife, am I?"

Her eyes widened, but she recovered quickly. "I wasn't certain what to expect. From what my husband and Mr McGregor said, I envisioned someone very young and delicate. Someone who would evidently need my help." Her smug expression said she believed she was right. William was hers, her eyes said, and I hadn't a hope of matching her.

Two could play at this game, and I suspected my political skills would be superior – after all, Mother had taught me to lead since I was a small child. In this case, compromise might be the key to conquest. If that's what it took to keep William out of her clutches, then so be it. "I admit I'd like your help on a few things. Such as, where does a girl go to get more dresses? I only left Fremantle with one steamer trunk and I've gone through half of my clothes in a matter of days."

"Singapore. The company sends us on the *Islander* to Singapore once a year and puts us up at that hotel…the Adelphi, I think it's called, though some swear by the Raffles, but I find the Adelphi far superior. A whirlwind trip of shopping that will make you feel like you're buying your trousseau all over again. Or, in your case, perhaps the first time."

I dismissed her jab with a smile and a wave. I wouldn't let her know that she'd guessed correctly and I had no trousseau to speak of. "The *Trevessa* sank so quickly there was hardly time to rescue luggage. Just getting all the people aboard into the lifeboats was challenging enough. I'm surprised William hasn't told you the story."

I was. He'd confided in the dragon in the Grotto, so I knew every detail of his harrowing ordeal in the lifeboat, from losing me to landing here. Yet he hadn't told those he worked with about the shipwreck? Not even his mistress. I felt a tiny ray of hope. No wonder he'd been so eager to have a confidante, even a mythical one.

"Perhaps over dinner tonight you can both tell your tale. About how you met and the terrifying tragedy of a shipwreck. You must join Jackson and I this evening for dinner "

I opened my mouth to say I'd need to ask William, then closed it again as I realised she'd already asked him and his response had been that the decision was mine to make, depending on my health. And there was nothing wrong with my health, except my own rampant libido.

"We'd be delighted to," I replied, then thought of the previous night's disastrous dinner with Jackson. "As long as you don't serve bat soup."

Anne choked on her tea.

One point to Mrs McGregor. I suspected I'd need a whole lot more to win William from his countrywoman's clutches, though. And I intended to play as hard as I knew how.

Thirteen

After I'd managed to get rid of Anne, I ventured back into the bedroom for a book. Not just any book – I wanted inspiration for thanking William for my motorcycle ride this morning. Something that could give him the same physical pleasure he'd given me, for I knew Anne was no match for me in bed. A few minutes and it was over, indeed. No wonder William had been so starved for sex.

I dug through my trunk, but I couldn't seem to find it anywhere, yet I remembered packing it. In fact, all of my books were gone.

Wait, hadn't I seen Captain Foster's book on the nightstand? William had been reading it and drinking whisky. I glanced at the nightstand, but there were no books there now, so I opened the little cupboard below it. Sure enough, someone had stashed all of my books inside. I pushed aside Captain Foster's book and the hefty volume of fairy tales Merry had given me. I wanted the little book bound in Moroccan leather that held secrets about sex in all sorts of acrobatic positions. The one I'd read and daydreamed about how much I'd like to do all of them with William. And, starting tonight, I would.

A sudden thought chilled my heart. Had he read this and tried some of the positions with Anne?

Even if he had, I'd be better at them, I resolved, tightening my grip. With my flexibility and strength, I was capable of far more in bed than any human. Hours, not minutes of pleasure. As I'd demonstrate to him tonight. I clutched the book to my chest and headed out of the dim room to find somewhere with better light for reading. The veranda, maybe? I thought I'd seen some chairs there. Perhaps there was still some jasmine tea left…

I made my way back to the dining room, where Amah had already started clearing the table.

"Yes, Mem?" she asked. "Help you?"

Help me? "Shouldn't I be asking if I can help you?" I reached for the plate that had held the shortbread and stacked it on top of another that was dusted with pastry flakes.

"No, Mem!" Amah pushed in front of me so I couldn't reach the table. "No, Mem!"

Cook came to our rescue. "Mem? Is something wrong?"

"I was just trying to help clear the table. I'm not used to…at home, I cooked and cleaned up after myself." My hands itched to be doing something, instead of lying idle while other people worked.

"Our job, Mem." Cook's eyes held sympathy, as if she'd had to explain this to other women in the past, and she understood my unease. "If we don't do our job, we are not paid and we must find other work. Your job is to please husband." Cook's gaze dropped to my book.

Had she read it? Did she know what was in it? Did she have suggestions?

I opened my mouth to ask.

Human women didn't discuss sex, and I'd promised William I would be the soul of propriety. Including…no, especially in front of his staff. And what if they'd heard him and Anne? I didn't want to hear about it if they had. Maybe Cook's sympathy was because she knew I'd met his mistress and I had a fight ahead of me for his affections. No, I didn't want to hear her say any more on the subject. As she said, my job was to please my husband.

I sighed and said instead, "Is there any tea

left? I wanted to take a cup out on the veranda while I'm reading my book."

Cook said something to Amah, who took a plate of tarts back to the kitchen. Then she turned to me, teapot in hand. "You'd like more tea, Mem?"

I nodded, defeated.

"I will bring a fresh pot to you."

Dismissed, I wandered out to find a seat.

Some time later, Cook set the tea tray on the table beside me. A wisp of steam curled up from the teapot, beside a single cup and saucer and a plate with two chocolate pastries on it.

"Thank you," I said, reaching for one of the cakes.

"You like éclairs, Mem?"

I pointed at the cakes. "Is that what these are? I don't know. I just like chocolate, that's all. William's fault. He gave me my first taste of chocolate soon after we met."

"Tuan likes chocolate?" Her eyes glinted. "These have bad custard. Not smooth. Too many lumps. Next time, I will make cakes for you and Tuan. Much better."

I snorted. There was rivalry between the Jacksons' cook and William's? Why was I not surprised? I'd be her willing ally in this, for a victory over Jackson's cook was also a blow to the pride of Jackson's unfaithful wife. "Only if you want to. I won't say no to chocolate. Especially not with William."

She headed back into the house and I returned to my book. Positions for kissing, ways to pleasure him with my mouth…ooh, that was just like the White House woman had done. I skimmed through the description, but it just didn't seem like enough. Mm, another night, perhaps. I wanted something more like the stuff of fantasy and dreams. I flipped through the pages and a dark stain caught my eye. The clear outline of my fingers in…ha. Chocolate. I'd been reading this in Merry's garden, dreaming of what I wanted to do with William, and my snack had melted under my hand. I felt a little flustered at the mere memory. Oh, this would be perfect… I continued reading.

"What are you reading, lass?" William nodded at my book as he trudged up the stairs.

I shoved it under the cushions. "Nothing important. Just waiting for you to come home…mmm." He silenced me with a kiss, though a chaste one. Was he thinking about Anne?

"Good thing I'm not much later, or you might have missed your first island sunset. What do you think?" He waved in the direction of the cliffs.

Was it truly that late? How long had I been reading?

Pink and orange streaks painted the sky behind the palm trees; a fitting backdrop for the sun sinking into the sea.

"I've seen brighter, more beautiful sunsets in Fremantle," I began carefully, "but this one is the best, because it's the first one I've seen from your side. A fitting end for my first day as your wife."

He flashed a tired grin. "The day's not over

yet, lass."

My heart leaped at the thought of going straight to bed to put my book-learned theory into practice.

"We still have dinner with the Jacksons," he continued. "And that Frankenstein film at the club." He offered me his arm. "We'll need to hurry and get dressed, then we can go and introduce you to the rest of island society."

Island society? More pointless protocol about inconsequential things like which dainty must be eaten first as Anne laughed quietly inside and her eyes brimmed with victory. Perhaps I should have been learning about the hierarchy of cakes instead of the joys of agile sex. Glumly, I headed inside.

Fourteen

"Oh my, I think that was the most frightening film I've ever seen. When that monster got loose and threw down young Mr Frankenstein's torch, I was certain he'd kill him for sure," Anne babbled, fanning her chest as if to emulate her fluttering heart. If she was trying to draw attention to her breasts, William hadn't noticed. Perhaps because my curves were definitely more generous.

I agreed with her assessment of the film, but for different reasons. The man's fighting skills had been so poor I could have overcome him with a well-placed kick. I was certain Anne had never seen a real fight, let alone been one of the combatants. Was this why she had time and thought for her cake protocol? Was her life so sheltered from reality that she'd never had to think of anything important? I tried to keep my thoughts from registering on my face. I'd faced worse monsters and fought them off – human ones, not something created by a madman.

"…and when he threw that little girl in the water, I thought of Jean and that time she was down at Isabel Beach. She stayed under much too long and I feared she'd drowned. I had Amah drag her out of the water and wouldn't let her swim again for weeks. She was just practicing holding her breath and diving, as she'd seen some of the Malays do, but…oh, remembering how terrified I was…"

"Jean's safe at school now," Jackson

muttered, but his words didn't seem to register with Anne. I wondered if she'd have listened to William if he'd interrupted her.

"…and when the monster showed up uninvited on their wedding day and attacked poor Elizabeth! Mr McGregor, what were you thinking? Choosing such a frightening film to watch with your new wife. I'm sure Maria is quite terrified that someone might try to hurt her or carry you off…why, you should be ashamed of yourself!" she declared, glaring at William.

"Perhaps you're right," he said shortly. He didn't even glance at her and my heart swelled with victory. Now he had me, she meant nothing to him.

She seemed to realise this, for Anne gave a nod and a sniff, before leading the way up the hill with Jackson trotting after her.

I stepped forward to follow, but William took my arm and we fell behind as I slowed to match his ambling pace. He was tired, I realised, and every step was an effort for him.

While I'd slept and slacked off for the afternoon, he'd worked as hard as I normally did.

"I'm so sorry. I did the same as that madman when I left you alone on the *Trevessa*. When I should have been protecting you from those animals. It wasn't a fiery windmill but the ship herself that foiled their dastardly plans. If the *Trevessa* hadn't sunk that night, I shudder to think what those animals would have done to you…"

I glanced at the Jacksons, but they were far enough ahead that they couldn't hear us. "I believe rape was what Sciarra and Barrett had in mind, William, before they planned to kill me. If they hadn't – "

William grabbed my shoulders. "They didn't. Lass, tell me they didn't. That the ship started sinking before they could…I thought I'd gotten there in time. There were two of them? I didn't see Barrett…he and Sciarra plotted to attack you together? What did Barrett do? And Sciarra? Lass, before I found you, did he…did they…"

Ah, I'd uttered a word that humans wouldn't say in polite conversation. Well, rape wasn't polite, but not mentioning it didn't make it go away. And I wouldn't lie to William about this.

"When I left our cabin, someone hit me and knocked me out. I didn't see who it was, but I woke up locked in the cargo hold. One full of that mud you'd warned me about. I believe their intention was to – " I glanced at William's expression and decided not to finish that sentence. His agony and guilt were written clearly across his face. Instead, I said, "Whatever their intentions, I wanted no part in them, so when Barrett came to the hold, I fought him. I'd already discovered a loose panel in the hull and when I dodged one of his blows, it scraped against the panel instead, knocking it free. Water came pouring in through the breach and he was right in front of it. I imagine he drowned, William, while I escaped to raise the alarm that the ship was sinking. While I was on my way to find you, I ran into Sciarra and…well, I'm sure you remember that part." I managed a sheepish smile that he probably didn't see in the dark. He'd come to my rescue, like the hero he was.

"My God," he whispered, tugging at his shirt collar as if it was suddenly too tight. "So it's my fault the ship sank, that you almost died, not just when I failed to protect you but — "

Anne's voice rang out sharply from the steps to the Jacksons' bungalow, "What are you two lovebirds whispering about? Hurry along! We won't wait dinner for you, you know."

It wasn't his fault, I wanted to say. None of it. The fault was mine. If I'd kept my temper in check and never been exiled; if I hadn't stolen the raft and instead swum away like a normal mermaid; if I hadn't fallen in love with William and joyfully shared his bunk that fateful night…

My life would be far lonelier for it. I wanted what William and I had, not some fishy future.

Even if my life included fitting in with catty society ladies like the sheltered Anne. And having to fight the silly woman for the man I loved. He was worth it. Whatever it took to win him from her, he was worth it. And I'd show her so during dinner. I could already feel victory within my grasp. She would never touch my husband again.

"We're coming," I called, leaning in closer to William before lowering my voice to add, "I still haven't thanked you properly for saving me from Sciarra, or for today's magnificent ride. Perhaps we should wait until after dinner, though?"

His expression softened slightly and he nodded before escorting me into the Jacksons' home.

Fifteen

There was no sign of the Jacksons' houseguests as we sipped our pre-dinner drinks on the veranda. I wondered if they'd be joining us for dinner.

"Such a delight to have one's house to oneself again. McGregor, sending the coolies up to the work camps was genius. Sheer genius!" Jackson lifted his glass to toast William.

"It was Maria's idea when she saw the empty camps this morning," William said softly, but I doubt anyone but me heard him. I smiled my thanks all the same.

"Dinner is served."

Jackson took my arm and led the way to the dining room, with William and Anne trailing in behind us. I gritted my teeth that Jackson would permit her to touch him, but he didn't seem perturbed at all. Surely he didn't think that I'd surrender William to her and I'd submit to him. Or didn't he know about his wife's indiscretions with William? I wrenched a chair out from under the table, determined to sit as far from Jackson as I could.

Anne stopped me before I could sit down. "No, Maria, you sit here beside me. Mr McGregor, on my other side, if you please. Can't have your husband monopolising you all night. Not when I want to talk to you!"

I opened my mouth to protest, looking to William for his support. He shook his head and took his indicated seat, nodding at the one across from him. Anne had won. A small victory, yes, but a victory nonetheless. I'd have to work harder to curb her influence over William.

At least it was only a tiny, square table, I consoled myself. I could still speak to him and see him, even if he was too far away to touch. I could restrain myself through a dinner, surely. And a siren's voice was her most powerful weapon.

"Mr McGregor, I declare your bow tie looks askew. I'm sure it was perfectly straight in the Club. What were you doing during the walk here to arrive in such disarray?" Anne leaned over and adjusted it, her hands lingering on his neck. "There. All fixed."

My blood boiled. How dare she touch William when he was mine? And I knew exactly when he'd shifted his bow tie — when I'd told him the *Trevessa* sank because of me. I should never have said anything. I should have kept quiet and not told him the trouble I had the power to cause. I needed to forget about the ocean and concentrate on being a good human wife. One who didn't have a tail or talk to dolphins. Or command sharks. Or kill the silly human woman beside me for her impertinence, no matter how much I longed to. No, I had to best her on her terms – human ones. That meant impeccable behaviour at dinner so that William would be proud of me.

Anne coughed, drawing my attention back to the present. She stared pointedly at my lap and I glanced at hers, then her husband's, for he sat on my left. He had a linen napkin smoothed across his lap. I presumed Anne did, too, but it blended into her dress so that I hadn't spotted it at first. My napkin sat rolled and alone on the table – William had his in place, too, I guessed. I snatched it up and spread the starched fabric across my skirt. I reminded myself to keep my wits about me.

A turbaned Indian man entered the room with a bottle in each hand, which he set down on the sideboard before he uncorked one of them with an audible pop. He poured a small volume of liquid into Jackson's glass and watched impassively as Jackson swished the wine around, sipped, then swirled the glass again and drank more deeply. Jackson's nod seemed to be some sort of signal, as the Indian man then filled everyone else's glasses, too.

We drank a toast to everyone's health, to the newlyweds – William and I, I presumed – and to good company, which was the last thing I expected to find here tonight. Unused to drinking much alcohol in Fremantle, as Merry hadn't been overly fond of it, it wasn't long before I could feel the slight buzz in my head from my drink. At least it wasn't foul, burning whisky, or that headache-inducing rum.

Two women appeared, carrying plates which they set down on top of the ones already before us on the table. Fearing that Anne would serve the same tasteless food that William preferred and I struggled to swallow, I glanced down with some trepidation and almost breathed an audible sigh of relief. Raw oysters sat beside a wedge of lime.

I pinched the lime between my fingers and squeezed the juice onto the protesting oysters. Humans couldn't hear their keening, but a quick glance at William made me wonder. Anne and Jackson looked equally uncomfortable, as if they, too, could hear the high-pitched sound. But William's lime was intact.

He caught my eye and pointed at a tiny fork before he lifted it and stabbed it into the lime, using it and a small knife to extract the juice and squeeze it over his shellfish. The others did the same and I felt my face reddening. There was not only a hierarchy of cakes, but a procedure for fruit.

Anne's tiny smirk told me she'd scored another point over me. I swore I wouldn't concede another.

I waited and watched the others before daring to touch my food again. If there was some secret to eating oysters, I needed to know it, but it turned out to involve nothing more than the tiny fork to loosen them before tipping the shell up at one's lips. This I could manage, I decided, though oysters weren't exactly my favourite seafood.

The first slimy beast slipped down my throat and I managed a smile before reaching for my wine to wash the taste down. One down, two to go. I thought I'd managed all right, only to find William frowning at me. I hadn't touched my next oyster, so it couldn't be that. I looked desperately to him for help.

He seized his wine glass, sipped much like I had, then carefully set it down precisely where it had been before. Ah…there was my mistake. I shifted my glass back to its original spot, hoping Anne hadn't noticed.

Her pursed lips told me this was a forlorn hope and I sighed inwardly, resolving to finish my oysters before venturing to drink any more wine. I slurped another oyster, earning myself a glare from Anne before she soundlessly tipped her last one into her mouth. Maybe William's whisky might have been a better choice — it could have burned my vocal chords into silence for the evening. I stared glumly at my lap.

Someone took the plate of empty shells away and replaced it with a bowl of clear soup.

"Ah, turtle soup. One of the coolies caught this big fellow this morning. His shell was more than three feet across!" Jackson boomed and I peered at my bowl in horror.

A turtle? A huge sea turtle? Didn't he know they lived longer than humans – as long as my people did? And three feet long…they made soup out of a century-old creature? My throat constricted at the thought of eating it, but I was the only one.

Much like Merry, they sipped it from spoons in silence, but I hesitated.

"Haven't you tasted turtle soup before?" Anne asked with a knowing smile.

I shook my head, unable to find words that would be polite enough for her table. They had no idea what manner of creature they were eating. What was wrong with their domesticated pigs and chickens?

"Oh, but you must, dear," Anne continued. "It's quite a delicacy. In England, it's only served on very special occasions, like engagements and weddings. Certainly appropriate for your first dinner party."

I remembered a much more relaxed dinner party with Tony at Merry's house in Fremantle. There'd been wine and fresh fish and comfortable conversation…oh, how I missed those days! But those days had been empty without William and I wouldn't return to Fremantle alone. No, I'd fight to remain at his side here. Whatever the price.

I glanced at William and capitulated to his imploring eyes. For him, I'd eat it. The poor beast was dead, after all – it would be a shame to waste it. Though each mouthful threatened to come right back up again, I spooned it up, heartily wishing I'd never agreed to Anne's dinner invitation. I wouldn't disappoint William in bed like I evidently was here at Anne's table.

When I'd emptied the bowl, I gulped down my mysteriously full glass of wine and let the alcohol blur the rest of the dinner party into a haze. I couldn't bear to see the pain on William's face or the forced smile on Anne's every time I made another societal faux pas. I'd lost him and he'd send me back to Fremantle on the first available ship, while he took refuge in Anne's willing arms. Better to take to the water than stay to watch that.

Sixteen

We waved goodbye to the Jacksons, who still stood on the veranda, and William's arm around my waist slid lower, lifting my spirits as we disappeared into the darkness. Maybe he'd forgive me for my bad behaviour during dinner.

"How's your behind after such a long ride today?" he whispered, caressing my bottom through my skirt as we crossed the garden to our house. He'd evidently consumed as much wine as I had – or perhaps it was the whisky he and Jackson had taken at the end causing him to slur his words a little.

"Aching for more," I replied, wondering if he meant the motorcycle or lovemaking. I wanted both, but as his stroking hand slipped under my skirt, the overpowering desire to take William to bed with me sent all thoughts of his Triumph out of my head. Anything to blunt the memory of this disastrous dinner.

"So am I. We'd best get to bed quickly, then." I caught the wistful note in his tone.

I smiled as I led the way inside. I'd memorised the chocolate-stained page of my book this afternoon and I had high hopes that I possessed the agility required to put theory into practice.

We made it to the bedroom and shut the door before decorum departed. I undressed him with eager hands, then made short work of my own clothes only to discover that he stood by the bed with his back to me.

"Lass, I'm dead on my feet, and in no mood for games after that dinner. Maybe you can…be a good wife tomorrow." He yawned widely and crawled into bed.

My heart sank.

A good wife. A good wife wouldn't have made such a mess of dinner and the least I could do to make it up to him was to agree to simple sex if that's what he wanted. Anything was better than none at all. How else could I compete with Anne?

I smiled and stretched out beside him on the bed, parting my thighs in eager anticipation.

"I had to work all afternoon after you wore me out, lass. And then that interminable dinner…a man needs rest," he said, rolling me onto my side and spooning up behind me. He pulled me firmly against his body.

I could feel him hardening at the close contact, so I wiggled closer, trying to arouse him further so we could make love like this, if that's what he wanted. I'd take him sideways, crossways or upside down just to feel him inside me.

"You don't need to tease me, William," I murmured, rubbing against him.

I heard a light snore in my ear as his grip slackened.

I swallowed my bitter disappointment. There would be no more lovemaking for us tonight, for poor William was too tired. Perhaps he wouldn't have been so tired if I hadn't agreed to the dinner party. So much for being a good wife. I was the worst wife William could have chosen. He'd send me home and return to his mistress for sure.

Seventeen

Sleep was a long time in coming. I ached with unfulfilled need and the crushing guilt that William would be better off with a human woman, instead of a creature like me. He hadn't even wanted my body tonight, when it was all I had to offer him. I resolved to take to the water and swim away while he slept. Then he'd be free to find a better wife – someone more suited to life on land. Or take up with his snippy mistress again, if she was who he wanted.

I slipped out of my nightdress and sneaked outside. Movement in the darkness told me where the Sikh jaga kept watch, but my night vision was better than any human's, so I slunk through the shadows and he didn't turn to look at me. I debated whether to head to the beach in the cove, but the splash of waves on the cliffs below tempted me too much. I broke into a run, soaring out over the water from the cliffs until I arced into the seething sea. Coolness embraced me, washing away perspiration and embarrassment and even my semblance of humanity as I shifted to my tail and opened my gills to the life-giving blue.

I dived and dived again, until I was too deep for even the island coral to survive. A shadow moved beneath me, more than twice my size. From the shape of its tail, I knew it must be a shark, perhaps searching for his dinner. I sang softly, warning him that there was only death in my direction. I was in no mood for kindness tonight.

The silly shark paid no heed to my warning, rising to the surface only feet from me, and I realised why. I'd underestimated his size. He wasn't a dozen feet long – more like thirty or forty feet, I guessed as the spotted whale shark cruised by. And hungry.

I tasted the water, noting the faint tang of his preferred coral spawn, but the cyclone could have carried it from anywhere. Yet some coral species took advantage of cyclones and summer storms, spilling their spawn into the swell so that it could be carried far and wide.

If anyone knew the whereabouts of spawning coral, it would be the spinner dolphins. I raised my voice and asked my question of the seas.

Those dreadful gossips couldn't resist answering, so mere moments passed before they responded: to the east and south around the point.

I called the shark and set off in the direction of his dinner. We were soon surrounded by glowing clouds of plankton, just as he desired, so I left the creature to feed as I wondered what to do with the rest of my night. I wasn't far from the entrance to my grandfather's cave — in fact, I could just make out the carvings around the opening.

I thought of returning to the Grotto, sleeping in the comforting arms of stone that had held me in hope, but I dismissed the idea. No, if I couldn't sleep in my husband's loving arms, then I needed to get as far away from here as possible before my resolve wavered and I returned to him. Yes, I loved him, but I wanted what was best for him, too. And that would never be me. Not if he didn't want me. I'd never be a good enough — I hadn't even lasted a day as William's wife. So much for love. It was just as Mother had taught me. We could never love a human, because they couldn't return our love. Better to be alone.

"Sirena! Elder Sephira looks for you! The Council commands your return with your child," a dolphin voice squeaked.

"Sirena, Sirena, come play with us. We found tuna!" said another.

The pod swirled and spun around me, churning the water before leaping above it. I could match their agility if I chose, but tonight's party had leached the joy from me. I didn't want to play and if I ate another thing I'd bring the rest right back up again, down to those sour oysters. At least there'd been chocolate at the end – the only consolation to a troublesome night with the Jacksons.

What I'd give to just share chocolate with William again, with no one else to interrupt or tell me off for eating with my fingers or the wrong fork or for making a sound when silence was required. Hierarchies of cakes and cutlery…who knew humans could be so complicated? Or that William would choose another woman over me because of such inconsequential things…

"I saw Elder Sephira yesterday, swimming not far from here. She will be excited that you are so near!" squeaked a young dolphin.

Mother? Here? My heart sank to the darkest depths.

A dolphin nosed my belly. *"Do you carry a calf yet? Elder Sephira promises rewards to the first to bring word to her that you are ready to return!"*

I pushed her away. *"No. I am not pregnant and you and Elder Sephira can stick your prying noses somewhere else."*

I stopped dead. Mother would come searching for me here. She might even harm William, as she'd threatened to hurt my friends in Fremantle. I couldn't leave William to her tender mercies. He was mine.

Leave the man I loved, the one I'd crossed an entire ocean for, to a weak woman who was someone else's wife? A woman who knew him as Grumpy McGregor, the cold man who ran the mine, and not the kind hero who heated my blood with desire and love? That would make me no better than the silly mermaid in a fairy tale. I was more than that. William was more than that.

I wouldn't surrender him without a fight. If

he preferred Anne to me, I couldn't let Mother kill him. No, I'd take his life with my own hands if it came to that. But I wouldn't allow it. William was mine, body and mind. I'd remind him that I had so much more to offer him than some sheltered human. The sex would be spectacular.

And maybe…maybe he'd even give me a child.

How did humans know when they were pregnant? I wondered. My people asked dolphins to check — no self-respecting healer would practice midwifery without at least one dolphin companion, though several was the norm. They could use sound to gauge the size and position of the child in the womb, something no human or mermaid could know without their help.

If my mother had offered a reward to dolphins for bringing her news…there was no way of stopping it. Dolphins were the worst gossips in the ocean, I knew well, though whales came a close second because their calls carried so much further. If a dolphin told a whale, soon the whole ocean would know that a wayward child had chosen obedience…

If I returned to Cocos, I'd be under the oppressive authority of the Elders. Ordering me around, making me comply with their societal rules. Even learning to live beside Anne was preferable to that. At least her rules allowed chocolate.

No. I would not capitulate to those vicious women. Not my mother. Not Anne. Not any of them.

I'd chosen a life on land and I'd damn well live it. With William, for as long as he'd let me.

Let me? Ah, but I wanted more than that. I longed to be his wife in truth, learning every bit of etiquette required to live on land at his side. And the only one who could instruct me was his mistress.

I needed to swallow my pride and ask Anne what to do. The last woman I wanted to speak to after tonight. I imagined she was already gloating at my ineptitude, so if I had to admit to her that I needed her advice, she'd surely be insufferable. But to best her at her own game, I needed her to explain the rules. And then I could rip William from her grasp forever.

I sped to shore. Tomorrow I'd try again to be William's perfect wife. Water knew I couldn't do a worse job than I had today.

Eighteen

When I woke the next morning, William was already gone. Not that the bed was cold. With the sun up and the humidity high, a wash with cold water was certainly in order. I dressed, combed and pinned my hair, then ambled to the dining room.

The table was set for breakfast, but there was no tea yet. Cook appeared from the kitchen at the sound of my footsteps on the creaky boards.

"Breakfast with Tuan in an hour, Mem. Would you like tea?"

"Yes, please." The house was stuffy and I wanted some air, so I added, "Can I have it on the veranda? Please?"

Cook nodded and I thanked her before heading out into the morning air. I chose the same chair I'd sat in yesterday, because it gave a good view of the road to the cove. I'd see William's approach first from here. My chair was less comfortable today, though, I discovered as I realised my book was still stashed under the cushions. Light reading for the morning, I decided. I'd want a new surprise for William in the bedroom tonight.

I emptied my teacup for the third time and I contemplated asking Cook for another pot of tea when a welcome voice called, "Good morning, lass. You look lovelier than the dawn today."

"William!" I flew down the steps and into his arms. He'd been in my thoughts all morning, given my reading matter, but it would take some time for the novelty of seeing him every day to wear off. I wished it could be this way for the rest of my life.

A chaste kiss was all he gave me, but we walked into the house arm in arm. I forced myself to maintain a similar reserve to his – William was surely ashamed enough at my behaviour last night. Or had he spent the morning with Anne? The very thought of her made me want to cry.

In an attempt to behave properly, I'd asked Cook to give me the same breakfast as William, so I tried to hide my chagrin at the less appetising smell of plain eggs and toast instead of yesterday's glorious omelette.

William didn't seem to notice the difference. "The call came over the radio this morning. There's a new engine for Ross Hill in Singapore and they'll be shipping it over on the next available vessel. I'll be out with a gang of coolies, laying a temporary rail line to the pump house all week. The sooner we get the engine in, the sooner we can start construction of new coolie lines at South Point."

"So you'll be headed out with the motorcycle?" I asked eagerly. "Can I come for a ride?" I'd found several positions that we could try in the water of the Grotto or on the back of the motorcycle.

William laughed. "No, lass. Coming for an inspection run is one thing, but a woman on a work site with so many men around? Hardly the place for a lady, let alone my beautiful wife. Send word to Mrs Jackson. I'm sure she'd be happy to introduce you to the daytime delights of the Club. Perhaps you can even play tennis."

Tennis? What in water was that? A card game of some sort? Something with more rules that I didn't know, so Anne could laugh at my limited knowledge? Not on your life. But it wasn't my life that depended on it — it was William's. And for him, I'd do anything.

I took a huge bite of my breakfast, and nodded. William didn't need to know my worries — this pump project sounded like it was troublesome enough without him knowing about the risk to his life. He didn't need to know that I planned to avoid Anne all day. Tomorrow, I'd swallow my pride ask for her help, but today I needed to nurse my wounds and plan how to seduce William when he reached home tonight. Let Anne enjoy her empty triumph for another day.

He wolfed down his breakfast and rose before I'd managed more than half of mine. "See you at dinner, lass. Best if you don't plan any dinner parties for this week, as I'll be out until daylight's gone. And I can't stand the damn things, anyway."

A quick peck on the lips was all the kiss I received before he headed off, pulling his goggles on.

I sighed and slowly finished my breakfast. I had more reading to do if I wanted to tempt William in bed tonight. Before he started snoring. And without a dinner party…perhaps I stood a chance.

Nineteen

My thoughts strayed to last night's fiasco and I found I wasn't reading a word from the book in my clenched fingers. I felt ill at the very thought of having to undergo another such ordeal today. Would Anne come and seek me out? Or would she avoid me because she believed I was beneath her?

I suppressed a snort. Beneath her on land was one thing, but beneath her in the water was far more dangerous than swimming with sharks. Sharks were predictable, driven by instinct, but angry mermaids could do almost anything. She'd better hope never to be in a boat when I swam below.

The snap of claws in the garden drew my attention. Two crabs squared off on the lawn while the corpse of a third, much smaller one lay in the grass beside them. Wonderful. Even the wildlife fought over food, though I doubted these were fighting over which fork to use.

I imagined the darker one as Anne and the lighter one as myself, though both were the bright red Christmas Island crabs I'd seen nowhere else. As they circled, I cheered the Maria crab on. No, not cheering, singing, I realised, as the fighting intensified. I'd spurred them to greater heights with the command in my song. But if my thoughts infused the song so much, perhaps I could calm them down by the same means. Willing Anne and Maria to cooperate and share a meal and a magnificent man like William without ripping one another's heads off…

A faint hope.

"Good morning, Maria. You have a lovely voice."

I stopped singing at the sound of Anne's voice. My return greeting stuck in my throat. It wasn't a good morning, not by a long shot. Instead, I nodded curtly. "Thank you," I bit out.

Her expression was a perfect mask of politeness. She didn't show a sign of the gloating joy filling her very soul. William was hers if I didn't act. If I didn't beg for her help. I'd never been brought so low in my life, yet when the reward was William's life, my sacrifice would be worth it.

I swallowed and swallowed again. "I…I'm sorry for my behaviour last night. I've never attended a formal dinner party before and I can't afford to embarrass William like that again. His position here on the island depends on me doing the right thing. Please…please can you tell me what I should have done?" My eyes beseeched her, filling with tears of dread at the triumph I knew I'd see in her eyes.

She closed her eyes and nodded, delaying the moment when I'd see her victorious expression. She opened her mouth and I cringed, expecting her to launch into the list of my inadequacies, yet she surprised me. "I brought a book you might like," Anne said. She ascended the steps and held the volume out to me. "It was a gift from Cora McMicken, the previous manager's wife, when I arrived. To this day, I don't know what I did wrong to alert her to my inexperience in society, but the book's been a godsend ever since. It will explain everything you need to know about afternoon tea, dinner and behaviour in situations I never thought I'd be caught up in until I arrived here. I think you need it more than I do now."

Reluctantly, I took the blue book and glanced at the title. Etiquette, by some woman named Emily Post. Grudgingly, I thanked her again and resisted the urge to throw her off the veranda.

"You should have seen your husband when he first arrived. Put milk in his teacup before tea every time. And getting him to dress properly for dinner has been an ongoing battle for years. Last night his bow tie was the closest to perfect I've ever seen it. He evidently puts in more effort for you," Anne continued, perching on the edge of the other veranda chair. She laughed gently. "When I saw his crooked tie last night, I couldn't help but try to fix it. I think it's the first time he ever stood still to let me – normally he'd have swatted me away. One glance at you calmed him, though, as if he'd do anything for you, including endure a straightened tie. He must have missed you a great deal while you two were apart. He couldn't take his eyes off you all through last night's dinner. He's been a bachelor so long, his weekly visits to the White House were quite a regular thing. Last night was the first time in years I didn't see him trudging down the road to the port after dark, because he had your company to look forward to instead. Last night at dinner, he looked like a man whose needs were causing him considerable pain." She winked. "I'm not surprised that you seem tired this morning. I wouldn't dream of suggesting tennis."

His mistress was a paid prostitute at the White House and not Anne after all? In fact, he never let her touch him? I let out a breath I hadn't known I was holding. "Thank goodness for that." Realising I couldn't explain the truth, I added, "I don't even know what tennis is "

Anne laughed as if I'd made a good joke. I didn't dare tell her that my words were in earnest.

"It's so lonely being the only European woman on the island," she confided in a low voice. "Perhaps now you're here I can leave the house more while Jackson's at work. Do you care for walking or bird watching?"

Not particularly, but it sounded better than warring with Anne over William or talking about what I should have done last night, so I hastily assented.

"Good," she replied. "Did you know there are three kind of frigate birds here at Christmas Island? And one of them is only found here."

Relieved, I listened to her lecture on the local birdlife, nodding at what I thought were appropriate intervals as she pointed to the birds riding the thermals above us. All the while, I wondered at her change of heart. Had I imagined her stiffness yesterday, or had something changed to soften her toward me sufficiently to offer friendship? Surely my crab-song couldn't be so powerful. How long had she been listening before she spoke? Long enough for the song to affect her?

I eyed the two crabs I'd watched earlier. Now, they were on opposite ends of their former colleague's carcass, clawing out their share of a meal.

Perhaps I'd been going about things the wrong way: the human way. Maybe being a siren was my key to becoming a successful society wife. Especially if a song had helped me win Anne over. I'd need to know precisely how to repeat the feat, though, and that meant practice. Plenty of it.

Twenty

Anne left to join her husband for lunch and I headed inside to do the same. The dining room was empty, so I entered the kitchen. Cook and Amah sat at the kitchen table, drinking tea and talking, and I felt like an intruder, even if I didn't understand a word of their conversation.

"Yes, Mem?" Cook asked, rising.

"I…I thought it was time for lunch," I said lamely, then added, "Not that I'm hungry, especially after the lovely morning tea you gave Mrs Jackson and I not long ago, but I thought William would be coming…" I trailed off as I recognised the sympathy in her eyes.

"Tuan took a packed lunch. He asked for a good dinner, for he will work hard today." She smiled. "There will be cake, Mem. Chocolate cake."

"Thank you." I wandered out again, disappointed that I wouldn't see William until evening. Was this what being a wife was about? Endless waiting for your man to come home? At least he didn't have a mistress I needed to worry about.

I sat down on the veranda, dangling my legs over the edge. I called the crabs out onto the grass once more, thinking to practice my singing on them for a little longer. If only I could call William as easily from across the island, but if he was at Ross Hill, he wouldn't hear a note of my song, however persuasive it might be. Instead, I had an attentive crustacean audience of three.

Okay. Time to start slowly, for I knew enough about siren song to understand that I could create dangerous consequences with nothing but my voice.

I had no need to practice calling creatures – I'd mastered that skill before I'd learned to shift from tail to legs. It was the first thing a child learned, so she could feed herself. Even land crabs came to my call and I think I'd even tried it on humans once, long ago on the *Trevessa* when I'd tried to call William and inadvertently summoned the whole crew to my side. If only I'd remembered the complement to a call – a dismissal – that night, but whisky had dulled my thought processes to the point where I'd forgotten. It worked on frenzied sharks, so it should be equally effective on humans, if not more so. Admittedly, my memories of that night are too fuzzy to recall much of what I'd sung at all, but the only explanation I had was that I'd called them. What else could I have done?

The other type of song all the girls of the

ocean's gift learned was one that enslaved: a song of control. We'd start with smaller creatures until a teacher or our matriarch deemed us capable of controlling something larger than ourselves. That inevitably meant a shark, for their simple, instinct-driven minds were easy to control. Once you controlled a creature, you could command it and it would obey. Duyong had taught me to ride the tiger sharks at Cocos, holding on to a dorsal fin as they darted through the reefs. This one we needed to master before we were allowed ashore, because it was our protection against humans. With humans, however, the orders could be more complex, because their brains were similar to ours. I could order a human to get me a drink, to make love to me, or to kill themselves, and they would. For that was the darker side of control: once a human knew what we were, they could not be permitted to live.

This death sentence was why I'd never attempted a song of control over those I cared about. Not Giuseppe, not William, not Tony and not Merry. I'd only sung once for William, and that had been my mother's soothing lullaby, not a song of power at all. And yet…William had been seasick until I'd sung it, and he hadn't suffered such illness since.

It was just a coincidence, I told myself. Nothing more.

Yet what had I been singing this morning as I watched the crabs fight? Some sort of call to arms, heightening aggression when my own fury threatened to boil over? Whatever I'd done, it worked, for the battle-lust I'd inspired had sunk the *Emden* when I was but a child. I'd riled Sciarra into a frenzy, too – though I'd been focussed more on driving the sharks into that state than some brutish human. Ah, but death had stalked the *Emden* that day and Sciarra hadn't survived long in the water with sharks, so I hadn't left witnesses to my songs of control then, for that's what I must have sung.

But this morning?

I leaned over and delivered the first notes of a song of control, barely audible to my ears and certainly too quiet for humans to hear. None of the crabs moved.

"*Run*," I whispered in the language of my people.

All three of them hurried off in different directions.

"*Stop and come to me.*"

The crabs resumed their usual, ambling pace and made their way back to the grass at my feet.

"*Fight.*"

They didn't move. Did they not understand? Then how had I managed to incite them to violence this morning?

I couldn't explain it. I sang a few more notes, releasing the creatures from my control, and they headed back to their hiding places in the garden.

So I hadn't controlled them this morning. It was merely a coincidence, as I'd thought.

But what about Anne's change of heart? Or

William's sudden sealegs? And why did the Elder Council and Mother in particular want me back so much? To share my secrets, such as they were?

Ah, it was too much for my head today. I needed a distraction, and as William's powerful body was nowhere near, I chose a book instead. Anne's infernal book of etiquette. That ought to occupy my mind for some time.

Twenty One

Etiquette occupied me for perhaps an hour until I was so bored I thought of feeding Emily Post's book to the crabs. I managed to restrain myself, though just barely, by tucking Anne's gift between the cushions of my chair and turning to my other etiquette book instead. I still hadn't chosen a position and I didn't want to be pulling the book out in the bedroom.

I wanted to try one of the methods of oral sex it spoke of, which the White House ladies seemed adept at, but I wasn't sure if William would be willing. Perhaps I should try something a little less adventurous…or at least memorise something else, in case I had to improvise quickly. One thing was for sure – Emily Post's book had nothing on the etiquette of whether one should pleasure one's husband with one's mouth. It seemed quite a serious lack, I thought. After all, if one etiquette book had such information, shouldn't they all? And the *Kama Sutra* predated Emily Post by a considerable length of time, so it wasn't as though it was a modern innovation.

I sighed. Human society was far too complicated. What had possessed me to want to conform to their protocols?

A familiar buzz caught my ears, faint but definitely approaching. Sunset light glinted off the metal as a motorcycle rounded the corner onto the dirt track to our home. I hurried down the steps to the yard, just as he brought his Triumph to a stuttering stop.

"William!" I cried, throwing my arms around him.

William didn't return my hug. Instead, he backed out of my embrace and headed toward the house. "Careful, lass. I'm covered in mud from today's fiasco. One of the tanks sprang a leak and caused a small landslide right where we were laying the track. I'll need to wash before dinner."

I glanced down. Too late – my dress was already streaked with mud, but I didn't care. William and I had spent far too much time apart. "I'll help you," I said eagerly as I followed him.

William led the way into a small room I hadn't seen before – a bathroom, though considerably more modern than Merry's bathroom on her back veranda in Fremantle. Unlike Merry's woodchip heater, this water tank smelled strongly of paraffin. But if the steaming water gushing out of it into the bathtub was anything to go by, it was far more effective than Merry's, too.

While I was distracted by the bath, William quickly stripped off his soiled clothes, dropping them in a waiting laundry tub. Ah, but then I had a much more enticing distraction. Rippled muscles defined him from head to toe as a man who worked long and hard for his living. And speaking of long and hard…

"If you want to help me, lass, you'll have to get out of that dress." He winked as he made short work of my buttons and threw my clothes on top of his. The moment I'd managed to shed my underwear, he scooped me up in his arms and deposited me in the half-full tub. The water splashed over the sides a little, then settled before he climbed in after me. Now the tub was full to the brim and quite crowded, too. "Come sit in my lap, lass."

I eagerly complied, stretching my legs out on top of his. He might not have been reading about sex all day, but he was no less eager than I was. Strong hands shifted my hips and he filled me with far more than warm bathwater. We made love slowly, but I relished every powerful thrust, wishing each moment could last forever. My breasts ached in his hands, nipples swelling from heat and passion and the sheer arousal of being so intimately entwined with William.

The pleasure of our leisurely joining built so gradually that I was moaning his name long before the first orgasm overpowered me, stealing my breath and my voice and anything else in the universe aside from my William. When I managed to open my eyes, I couldn't stop shaking from the adrenaline of such an overwhelming release. William had stilled, but I'd been vaguely aware of him reaching his peak even as I flew to the pinnacle of mine.

"I love you, lass," he said hoarsely in my ear. "My perfect wife. I'd gladly work every day in hellish mud if I knew I could come home to you and this glorious…you."

I was still too breathless to speak, but I knew what I wanted to say. That I'd give up the ocean and any chance of a position as Mother's heir on the Elder Council, just to spend the rest of my life with William on land as his wife. Learn etiquette as well as Anne knew it to be the wife he wanted. It didn't matter what the rest of the island or the world thought of me, as long as I was good enough to be William's wife. And I could say none of it.

Instead, I pressed his hands harder against my breasts, feeling my racing heartbeat and knowing he could, too. This was love, the all-consuming desire to do anything for the object of my love, whatever the cost to myself. All I wanted was William, now and forever. "I love you. You are my world, William." I tipped my head back so I could kiss him.

We only broke the kiss as a knock sounded at the door, followed by Cook's voice: "Dinner is ready, Tuan."

"We'd better get out and get dressed, then," William grunted. Reluctantly, I followed him out of the bath.

Twenty Two

I did my best to remember all that I'd learned from Emily Post about formal dinners while we ate and my efforts earned me a smile from William as I dabbed the last hints of chocolate icing from my lips with the napkin.

"Are you tired tonight?" I asked carefully.

He regarded me as intently as I did him. "I would like to go to bed early." He dismissed Cook and Amah with a wave as he rose.

"With me?" My voice quivered with uncertainty. What if he rejected me again? Had our brief coupling in the bath been the best I could hope for?

William glanced around, but we were alone. In two strides, he reached my side and scooped me out of my seat. "Of course with you, lass. You're my beautiful wife. I don't want anyone else as much as I want you. I've been looking forward to this all day and the bath was just…an aperitif."

He carried me out of the dining room and straight to the bedroom, depositing me in the middle of the bed. "You won't need those clothes any more, lass." He swiftly undid his shirt buttons and bared his torso.

I climbed off the bed and stripped, my smile widening at William's evident admiration. Maybe…maybe I could be a good wife to him after all. His ardent kiss certainly told me I wasn't doing too badly so far tonight.

When he tried to edge me back onto the bed, I shook my head and pointed at the cane armchair in the corner.

"Trust me," I murmured. "I want to try something special tonight."

I pushed him onto the seat and crawled into his lap. Concentrating through his kisses became a challenge, particularly as his hot length hardened underneath me, tempting me to give up on my exotic plans and simply ride him to bliss as we were.

Maybe later, if I failed at this, I told myself, and lifted one leg over his shoulder, then the other, framing his face between my calves. I took a deep breath, wondering if I could manage the rest.

"You're killing me, lass. I have to – "

I cried out as he surged into me, filling and heating my insides like lava. I wanted to lean forward to kiss him, but another powerful thrust threatened to take away my self-control altogether. I forced myself to lean back until my spine lay between his legs, my head resting on his shins. He grabbed my arse to stop himself from sliding out at the same time as I seized his thighs, ramming him as deep inside me as he could go. I arched my back, sliding slowly up and down his length until I almost screamed in frustration as the friction pushed me closer and closer to the edge without tipping me over.

"Bloody book," I swore, wanting to pitch it in the ocean for instructing me so poorly. If there'd only been pictures…

"Book?" William said. "Ah, if it's the one I think, you'd better let me take command."

William didn't wait for a reply. He yanked my legs down his sides, so his arms rested on top of my thighs, then fastened his hands around my arse again. "You might want to put your hands on the floor to keep your balance."

My hands slapped onto the floorboards as he hauled my hips higher, changing the angle before he asked, "Are you ready, lass?"

I nodded once and moaned as his next thrust sparked all my nerves on the way in. And again. Each time he dived inside me, it was as if a flame flared brighter, setting me alight. My orgasm broke over me in a wave of blinding brightness as I screamed for joy.

So much for his metal machine or the call of the sea. William was the ride of my life and nothing would tear us apart.

Twenty Three

When you hardly see your husband and the only thing you do together in bed is sleep, the *Kama Sutra* is about as useless as a motorcycle to a mermaid. Well, most mermaids.

For me they were both fodder for fantasy. Dreams of what I wanted to do…once William was done with all the rebuilding brought on by the recent cyclone and landslide. The Ross Hill pumping station was now connected to a spur rail line, though it required constant maintenance to keep the line above the sucking mud. The design for the replacement pier was complete, awaiting only the building materials and calm ocean in the cove to commence work. The new houses at South Point weren't William's problem – they'd be the South Point manager's responsibility, but William still needed to ensure the building materials made it from the port to South Point between the delivery of the new Ross Hill pumping engine and all the phosphate travelling between the mine and the port.

We could see the ship carrying everything we needed just drifting offshore, waiting for the swell in the cove to die down so it could unload the construction materials William needed for this ambitious schedule of works. If only sirens could calm storms…

For a moment, William was silhouetted against the faint light coming in through the doorway. All hardness and muscle, just begging to be kissed and caressed. But all I received was a peck on the lips before he pulled on his shirt and hid his gorgeous body from me. I thought I caught a glimpse of a shadow on his side, like a bruise, but it could have been just a trick of the light. I'd fallen asleep waiting for him last night, so I hadn't seen him undress. Perhaps tonight, if all went well, we'd be at leisure to explore each other's bodies in intimate detail. Just as long as that bloody ship docked today.

By the time I'd risen, William had vanished down the road to Flying Fish Cove. The weather report and any communication from the drifting ship would be waiting for him in the wireless station, and he'd hopefully share any news with me over breakfast. I dressed and pinned up my hair in the pre-dawn light, knowing Anne would comment if I wasn't looking my best. I left off my hat and stockings — that was one item of correct attire I hadn't bothered with. Who'd want to wear stockings in the tropics? Certainly not me.

Anne had lent me some books to read, as I'd exhausted William's collection during my first fortnight of lonely mornings. Today's volume was from a man named Rudyard Kipling, who'd lived in India. I found his accounts of colonial life there fascinating, as they weren't dissimilar to everyday life here on Christmas Island, but I did find him quite obnoxious, too. That meant I read through his books quite quickly and today was no exception. I closed the book with a snap and headed back inside for an old favourite – the book of Hans Christian Anderson fairy tales Merry had given me as a going away present.

I'd no sooner settled in my seat on the veranda when Cook appeared with a tea tray, the faint scent of jasmine wafting out to wish me a good day.

I smiled, thanked Cook and wished her a good morning.

"Not such a good morning if the supply ship doesn't come in. We have only tea enough for one day, maybe two," she grumbled and I realised why my tea didn't smell as strongly as it usually did. Rationing, I presumed.

"That means we're low on food, too, doesn't it?" I asked.

She grinned. "Plenty of eggs, chicken and pork, with vegetables from the garden, but there will be no bread or tea tomorrow."

I was the reason for this, I was certain, though she didn't say it. I'd been drinking her tea supplies and eating far more of William's food than their last grocery order from Singapore had allowed for, but I also knew she'd been shopping at the kongsi, the Chinese grocery store, to purchase more. I assumed even the kongsi had run out of tea, given how much I'd been drinking. As for flour for bread…even I knew that had to be ordered from Singapore.

I'd happily head out to sea for fresh fish instead, but mealtimes were the only time I saw William, and sometimes not even then. Last night he'd missed dinner altogether. The third night this week I'd dined alone. I'd almost wished for another disastrous dinner party with the Jacksons if it meant company, but I couldn't quite bring myself to suggest it. Even if I did think I'd only make half as many mistakes as last time.

I opened my mouth to apologise, but she'd already returned to the house. I opened Merry's book to the tale that mesmerised me most – the one about a young mermaid who wanted to be human.

Why it held my attention so much, I couldn't say. Of course, there were parallels in her story and mine, given we both left the ocean to live among humans, but that's where the similarities ended. She'd given up everything, even her voice, to catch the man she wanted. I'd had everything taken from me and I'd gained a voice, in learning William's language. She'd never known a man's love, nor had she loved one – her prince was just a means to an end. And she'd seriously considered killing the man she purported to love, perhaps the most sensible thing she did in the whole story, given that he'd utterly rejected her for some other woman despite the tortures the poor mermaid had endured. But her intelligence was short-lived and she not only let the man live, but ended her own life, too. Ah, no, her final thought had been rational – she'd thrown her dying body into the ocean, instead of leaving it for humans to examine.

I couldn't even contemplate killing William – I loved him too much for that. And I knew he returned my love. No, I'd never cast myself back into the ocean. Not now I'd lived with him and known the joy that was our life together. If happiness meant remaining on land and pretending to be human, so be it. No human had even guessed at my true nature in all my time on shore – not even Merry, who'd lived with me for years, and William didn't believe in mythical creatures. No, I would be the perfect, human wife for William until the end of our days. William and I had been apart long enough and I wouldn't permit the ocean to separate us again.

A soft, "Breakfast, Mem," roused me from my thoughts and summoned me into the house. Somehow, the sun had risen and the frigatebirds were fishing in the waves for their breakfast, so it shouldn't have seemed like such a surprise that it was time for mine. And William's.

Rationing meant I was back to Cocos eggs, I was pleased to see, as William barely noticed if I'd decided to eat raw robber crab for breakfast, let alone an omelette with shrimp. The appetising aroma alone was enough to make me ravenous, and in the absence of anyone to censure me for unladylike behaviour, I cut myself a large piece of omelette that barely fitted in my mouth.

"It's a ruddy miracle. The cove's as flat as a millpond this morning and we've already winched the engine ashore!" William burst into the dining room, grinning with the best news we'd had in weeks. "I have to return right away to head up the incline with this load. Get Cook to send some lunch up later. I'll see you at dinner, lass!"

I received a peck on the cheek and a shower of crumbs from his mouthful of toast, and my husband was gone before I could say a word.

Sighing, I reached over and snagged his unwanted slice of toast. If the ship in the port wasn't the *Islander*, it would be a while before I saw more bread. It'd be a shame to waste it.

Twenty Four

After breakfast, armed with a fresh pot of distinctly weak tea, I sat on the veranda for singing practice. Not that I improved any, but some siren I'd be if I lost my voice.

My consortium of crabs assembled at the first notes of my call now – almost as if they'd been trained to respond, too. I worried that I was eroding their natural instincts in driving them to obey me so frequently, but it was better to test this on six crabs out of that many million on the island instead of enslaving humans. Well, I thought so – Mother and the other Elders might not agree.

A light song of control soon had them even more attentive, responding to simple commands as easily as breathing. One command had never worked, but I still tried it. "Fight," I whispered.

They sat unmoving, lined up in front of William's motorcycle. Usually he rode the Triumph to work, but today he'd taken the train, so here it stood. I started to sing the sequence that released the creatures from my command.

I was tempted to offer to take William's lunch to him on the motorcycle, but I'd only ridden it once and William had been my passenger, shouting instructions or simply reaching past me to take control, the whole way. I wanted more riding lessons, but those would have to wait until William had time for me again.

What sort of job required such hours from a man? Day and night without cease or rest, barely stopping to sleep and no time to spend with his wife. And was the shadow I'd glimpsed this morning bruising from some injury suffered at work? I'd heard rumours of riots when the coolies had been worked too hard or their supervisors had used violence. This was why we had the ever-present Sikh guards in the Settlement and on watch outside our homes. But if someone had hurt William, I would not be content to sit idle. I'd summon tiger sharks to the cove and watch them feed on the culprit's sorry carcass. While he was still alive.

The crunch of metal drew my attention and I gasped in horror. The crabs had begun to attack one another and, much worse, William's motorcycle. They'd already shredded the tyres and one particularly feisty creature had climbed up the frame, snipping wires and lines with its claws as it went. A robber crab's claw reached up and severed the fuel line before attacking the fuel tank itself.

"Stop, stop!" I cried, jumping off the veranda to shoo the beasts away from William's crippled Triumph. They paid me no heed – they were too busy destroying things. Something nudged my foot and I turned to see another robber crab with its claws raised, ready to join the fray by ripping through me.

I stamped my foot – usually sufficient to drive the huge crabs away – but the claws rose higher still.

Hesitantly, I began singing again – a song of control, though I could hear my voice shaking. I just wanted them to stop wreaking havoc, to calm down and go back to their usual hiding spots. I wanted no more violence.

The sound of ripping metal stopped. I dared to open my eyes. Both of the robber crabs were backing away into the shadows beneath the house, one still clutching a glinting piece of metal from the motorcycle. The red crabs scattered more slowly, but their holes were nearer. Even as I watched, they disappeared.

From four to two to one to…no, they were all back in hiding. I let out a little moan of relief.

I was under no illusions. I'd done this…somehow. With a misguided song, I'd driven the controlled crabs into a frenzy. I'd even incited the two hidden robber crabs to riot. But why had they fought now, instead of when I commanded them to? And why the robber crabs, when I'd only controlled the red crabs?

I wished the memories of the party on the *Trevessa* weren't so hazy. What had I sung to drive them to my side? It wasn't a song of control, for the somnolent look and slow response of those under command made them unmistakeable. It was as if I'd somehow imbued my own emotional state into the melody, transferring my desires to my listeners and driving them to respond. So when I'd sat in the mess hall, quietly singing along with the gramophone as I wished for William to return, the room full of men had responded by offering to take William's place. And when I'd raised my voice on North Keeling Island as a child, furious at the humans who'd murdered Duyong, I'd wanted nothing more than for them to slaughter each other, which they had.

And now? I'd thought of rioting and violence, shredding a body into tiny pieces, and the crabs had responded, taking their fury out on William's poor Triumph. That clinched it. It wasn't safe for me to sing around humans – or to sing at all, without a clear purpose in mind. If that was what I needed to live safely on land without hurting those I loved – or their prized possessions – then so be it. I'd never sing again, silencing the siren inside so I could live happily as a human. It wasn't such a sacrifice, surely.

My tongue would be busy enough when William got home: trying to explain what had happened to his motorcycle. Luckily, he wouldn't believe the truth.

Twenty Five

The trudge of footsteps on dirt alerted me before Anne's voice rang out: "Time for your tennis lesson!" She stopped dead. "What on Earth happened to your husband's motorcycle? Did the coconut crabs get to it?"

I closed my book. "Yes. They were…unusually aggressive this morning. Two of them. I managed to chase them back under the house, but not before they did a fair bit of damage. I hope William can fix it."

She bit her lip. "I doubt it. He'll probably need to get a new one. You should push him to take you with him. You haven't been shopping in Singapore yet and you really should."

I glanced down at my dress, which was one of three morning dresses I owned. I'd have called them work dresses before, but they were looking distinctly worn after the beating they took in Amah's laundry, and I wasn't sure how many more they'd survive. My clothes certainly were cleaner than they'd been after a round in the laundry with me, though, to give Amah her due. A welcome distraction caught my eye and I reached for Anne's book. "I should get some new books there, too. Here – I've finished with Kipling. He's very pompous. I hope he never comes to the island to visit, especially if he speaks like he writes. I'm not sure I could keep a straight face."

"Once you start laughing, you'll set me off, too, so we're both lucky he'll never visit

Christmas Island. No one, not even Mr Murray, the CIPCo manager, deigns to visit us." She pronounced the abbreviated company name as though it was one word. "Leave the book here. Kipling's no use at tennis. I'll pick him up on my way home."

We strolled down to the wide, grassy expanse of the padang, where some of the kampung children were waiting to act as ball girls and boys for our game. The first time they'd been there I'd protested, not wanting to be embarrassed in front of a group of children, but I'd found tennis to be a matter of force, angle, control and momentum – all the parameters I used intuitively while swimming. I believe humans called this physics and it was best understood by engineers like William, or so Anne said, but it was one of the first lessons my kind learned as children, for judging the ocean currents and eddies poorly could kill more surely than any shark.

The children were necessary to ensure we didn't lose all our tennis balls. The crabs mistook them for eggs and stole them, so the children rescued our balls from the crustacean kidnappers and earned themselves credit to spend on sweets at the kongsi, courtesy of Anne and I.

Today I focussed fiercely on the game, trying to keep my mind on the ballet of ball, racquet and…"That benighted bosunbird took the ball!" I cried in surprise, watching the golden bird soar across the padang and into the jungle, its long tail streaming behind as if taunting me to take hold and drag the bird back. Luckily for him, the bloody bird flew too fast and too high for me to catch it.

Anne doubled over laughing. It took her some time to recover her composure, by which time she'd called an end to our game, declaring me the winner. Linking her arm through mine, she set off up the road. "We should have lunch together today. The men are all up at Ross Hill, playing with trains and engines and heaven knows what else, so we'll support one another and perhaps even have a glass of wine to celebrate."

We headed for her house, where one glass of wine multiplied into several – I lost count after the third – and we only switched to tea because we'd finished the last bottle of wine. Supplies truly were running low if the Jacksons were out of wine.

Two pots of tea later, I wove my way somewhat soberly through the garden that separated the Jacksons' bungalow from ours. I could already hear the train cars coming down the incline in the cove, so William couldn't be far from home.

I trudged up the steps, surprised at how heavy my legs felt. Had I done too much exercise during our tennis match?

A shadow in my reading chair shifted. "I thought you'd be home by now, lass," William said, rising.

"I was with Anne. We fell to talking and lost track of the time," I replied, crossing the veranda in three strides so I could dive into his open arms. I inhaled the scent of him, wanting to burrow into his chest as his arms wound around me. He smelled of soap, not mud and paraffin and machinery. I raised my head so I could see his face. "Have you already bathed? You've been home that long?"

"It's a good thing you've made friends with Jackson's wife. I thought you two didn't get along at first, but I guess I was wrong. As for my bath, I came down the incline with a load of phosphate. I wanted to show you that you still have a husband under all the grime, for I was afraid you wouldn't let me in the house otherwise." William's chest rumbled with his chuckle before he dropped his voice to a whisper. "And I figured if I was clean, it was more likely you'd agree to do some dirty things in bed tonight."

It was my turn to laugh. "I'd love to." With my body pressed against his, I could feel his eagerness, and it matched my own. "Before dinner or after?"

His stomach rumbled. "After, lass. I've had naught but sandwiches all day, so I hope you've ordered a good dinner."

I just smiled. Me, order Cook around? She knew what she was doing and the kitchen was definitely her domain. "I should dress for dinner." Despite my words, I didn't want to leave him, even to go into the next room.

"You look beautiful just as you are. And if I have to see you undress, we'll never make it to the table," William replied, offering his arm.

I thought of taking him to bed anyway, but I could wait an hour or two until we'd eaten. William was certainly worth waiting for.

Twenty Six

"How do you feel about a short holiday in Singapore?" William asked, popping a piece of pork into his mouth.

"I've never been," I admitted. He didn't mean to send me alone, did he? "I hope you'll show me all the sights."

He laughed. "I don't know about sights. The only thing I ever do in Singapore is business and shopping. If you want to do more motorcycle riding with me, we'll need to get you some more appropriate clothes. You can get those in Singapore."

Motorcycle…oh. I squirmed in my seat, not wanting to mention the mess I'd made today.

"I'll need to pay a visit to the motorcycle shop there, too. Damn crabs destroy everything. Last week we discovered a section of rail line that had sunk a good four feet because of the crab burrows beneath it. Good thing the new engine didn't come in before we'd filled that or it'd never have made it to Ross Hill. It seems we're at war with the crabs. First the train lines, then my Triumph…they're cutting the transport lines. Do you think they might be conspiring with the sea dragon to keep the weather so bad that no ships can dock, either?" William laughed. "Dragons that can control the weather. Sounds like one of the tales the coolies tell after they've been smoking too much opium. A battle here would be short-lived. We have no troops, no weapons and if they brought in reinforcements by sea…the island would be taken in no time. Good thing the Great War's over and there'll never be another, eh, lass?"

I smiled wanly, struggling to swallow a piece of potato that was suddenly too dry and stuck in my throat. "I hope not."

Cutlery clattered as William reached for me, enfolding my hands in his. "I'm sorry, lass. I forgot you saw action here when you were a child. The *Emden* attacked and then burned. A battle you'll never forget, I'm sure." He seemed to realise he'd said too much, so he changed the subject. "Enough about war. Let's talk about our trip to Singapore. The *Diomed*'s finished unloading and she'll be shipping out tonight. The *Islander* should dock in the morning, if this calm weather holds. She'll stay in port for a few days and when she leaves, we'll be aboard. How does that sound?"

"A holiday with you sounds lovely," I admitted, breaking into a proper smile. After all, a holiday meant no work, so I'd get to spend all my days and nights with William, just as we had on the *Trevessa*.

He dabbed his lips with his napkin and threw it on the table. "How about we skip dessert tonight and head straight to bed?"

My heart leaped. "That sounds even better. I'll just ask Amah to fill the hot water heater for me before she leaves, then. I won't be long."

Twenty Seven

I hurried to the bathroom, undressing as I went, intending to wash quickly and make it to bed before William had finished his after-dinner glass of whisky. A swift glance in the mirror turned into a longer look of horror, though, as I realised that after my hair had been crushed and steamed under a hat all day, I needed to wash it. I ripped out the pins, throwing them into the washbasin, before turning on the bath taps. The hot water was a little over lukewarm, but I didn't have time to wait. If I had to choose between a hot bath and a hot night with William, William would win every time.

I scrubbed at my scalp, freeing my tresses so that I could try to comb the tangles out. This was where I'd normally ask William for help, but I wanted his hands to be involved in far more intimate caresses. I yanked the comb though my hair a few more times, hoping I'd caught all the knots, before I gave it one more rinse and drained the bath. A cursory drying with the towel and I deemed myself ready. I hadn't brought a robe, but with only William and I left in the house, it didn't matter. It's not as though I wanted to hide my naked body from him.

I padded across the floorboards, my anticipation building as I saw the dining room light was out. William waited for me in the bedroom, then. I paused in the doorway to take a deep breath, knowing this showed my breasts to their best advantage, before sauntering to the bed.

"William? How would you like me this evening?"

He didn't move, so I leaned over to see his face better. Damp tendrils of hair landed on the pillow beside him, but William didn't wake. He just scrunched his nose up at a droplet that had fallen on his face before starting to snore.

Not again. This damned mine would work him to death.

Disappointed, I plaited my hair into a loose braid and climbed into bed beside him. His bare skin against mine was some consolation, at least. Soon, I promised myself, we'd go to Singapore and share all our time, in bed and out of it. And we could share our fill of sexual pleasures, too.

Twenty Eight

I blamed William's glass of whisky and my silly desire for human hygiene. I wanted him so much and it was immensely frustrating to be so close to him and yet not be able to make love. Again. I waited until I could stand it no longer, then slipped out of the house for a swim, the only thing that could extinguish the roaring blaze of my ardour. My last one, I promised myself, before I forced myself to forget about my former life and focus on being human.

I wondered what humans did when they were frustrated in their desires for sex. It's not a subject I'd ever heard discussed, but surely it had to happen. Who to ask, though? Not Anne, and certainly not William, because he'd only apologise and feel terribly guilty. If I were in Fremantle, I'd have asked Merry. She'd have blushed, as she had through every page of the *Kama Sutra* when she'd taught me to read, but she'd have answered. As a widow who had no lover, she must know. I resolved to write to her. I hadn't even told her that I'd found William yet, so a letter was long overdue, I mused as I splashed through the shallows of the rocky beach.

The cove was empty, but I could see the dark shape of the *Islander* just offshore near Smith Point. Another huge shadow drifted further out — a phosphate ship, I presumed, waiting to load up. Good thing I wouldn't be swimming any more, then. Loading phosphate unleashed clouds of dust into the air and water, which floated as a thin layer of brown scum on the surface of the waves. Not to mention it got into gills and lungs alike, making it difficult to breathe no matter what form I took.

If this was my last swim, then I'd take my true form, I decided, undulating my body through the water until I felt the stretch of skin covering my thighs, my calves and then past my toes, sealing them together into a tail that rivalled those of the dolphins I could hear playing in the open ocean. Or the whale shark making his ponderous way into the cove in search of me, though his was much bigger.

"*Where is the best plankton today*?" I called to the dolphins.

A cacophony of voices directed me through a maze of rocks, reefs and tasty fishing spots to a location I vaguely recognised as just off Jackson Point, the north-west most point of the island. It wasn't named after Anne and her husband, she'd told me laughingly when I asked, but after a different Jackson who'd designed the pier that the cyclone had carried away. With William designing its replacement, I wondered if they'd call it McGregor Point instead, or whether someone would name a different feature after him. I fancied McGregor Grotto. Perhaps I should mention it to the District Officer next time I saw him in the Club. He was due to be replaced soon, so it would be an appropriate recommendation for his final report.

Human concerns, the naming of things that would long outlast anyone who remembered the ephemeral title of the place. My laughter at my own silliness bubbled up to the surface. I truly was becoming more human than siren, if I even thought like them. I beckoned to the whale shark and led the way around Smith Point.

A pod of spinner dolphins joined us as we rounded the outer reefs that sheltered the northern beaches from the surf, squeaking their delight at seeing me again.

I tensed as I heard their rebounding calls, the sounds they made to gauge depth and obstacles and sense their way through the water. They could determine much smaller floating bodies with these calls, I knew, for Mother had utilised their talents during several births of our kind. They could judge the size and positioning of a child in a womb – or its presence before even the mother knew of it. If I carried a child, William's child, I couldn't hide it from them, however much I wanted to.

"Plenty of fish today," the oldest dolphin told me with considerable satisfaction.

"Not as many as Sephira the Elder will give for news of Sirena's child!" a youngster chirped, soaring out of the water and spinning a somersault before her elder could reprimand her.

I ached to ask if I carried a child, but I forced myself to remain silent. I didn't want to remind them to check, if they hadn't already. A faint hope, but a hope nevertheless, that Mother didn't know my whereabouts and I'd be left alone to my happy life with William. My happy human life.

"*Elder Sephira asks for regular reports for the Council,*" the old dolphin continued. "*I think she will not be content with hearsay for long. She is a mother and she misses you, as she should.*"

"*Mother does not miss me. She wants me to take her place on the Elder Council so that she can retire to carp at me every day,*" I snapped, remembering her endless lectures stretching back to my earliest memories. "*The rest of the Council don't care for me. Not after I told them to…*" Disappear up their own fundamental orifices, I think was the rough translation, though I wasn't going to repeat the crude vernacular to a gossip-mongering dolphin. My words would be all over the Indian Ocean by morning.

"*A mother knows what her child is capable of, especially when her power is great already,*" the dolphin said smugly and I stopped dead.

Did she mean that Mother knew what my voice could do…and any child of mine would be equally powerful? She wouldn't be content with taking one child from me – she'd steal any child of William's, too. And teach them to enslave humans…

I couldn't let that happen. I'd lock myself in a cage on land to keep from falling into Mother's hands – me and any children I might have. This swim was a mistake. I needed to return to land.

"I will leave this place soon. I must…must go and get ready," I blurted out, hoping it would be enough to deter Mother from searching the island for me.

I commanded the dolphins to take the whale shark to where they'd said the best plankton was, and hightailed it home.

Human. I had to pretend to be human for the rest of my days. I'd never shift to my tail and swim again, I thought as I stumbled up the beach at Flying Fish Cove and my home.

Twenty Nine

If I thought I'd barely seen William before the engine arrived, I was mistaken. He left before I was awake in the morning to ride the freight train out to South Point; he no longer returned for breakfast and when he finally trudged home at the end of the day, he was too tired to even eat dinner. Or if he did manage to eat, he wasn't capable of conversation. I'd seen more of him when he'd thought I was the dragon in the Grotto. Perhaps if I turned my tail in bed he'd notice me…

I glanced at the sleeping man beside me. No, not even then. He worked too hard and he'd more than earned a holiday. As long as he didn't sleep through the departure of the *Islander.*

My steamer trunk was packed, as was his, and some men would come to collect them in the morning. This time tomorrow night, we'd be aboard and waiting for her to leave. And, if I had any say in the matter, we'd also be in bed…but there wouldn't be any snoring for many hours yet.

I was too excited to sleep. I knew a swim would calm me – slicing through the waves, letting the cool water soothe me with its motherly caress – but I was true to my vow. The ocean was outside the bars of my invisible, self-imposed cage, and I would not leave it. Not if it meant losing the shelter of William's comforting arms, which still held me when he was fast asleep.

As I lay there in his embrace, I thought of what I might write in a letter to Merry. That I'd found William and agreed to be his wife, certainly. Perhaps a little about island life. Or should I include more? Fill my letter with happy anecdotes about my perfect life as a Mem on Christmas Island and not bother her with my worries? Or pour out my heart, telling her about the difficulties of being the wife of one of the island's Tuans, the men in charge, who put in so many hours it was like losing him all over again, for he was never home. Not knowing what signs to look for to see if I was pregnant.

What I'd give to be able to ask the dolphins, but I couldn't risk them betraying me to Mother. Being born as the daughter and heir of the most powerful Elder in the Indian Ocean was a curse I wouldn't visit on anyone. Certainly not my daughters. Mother could command the Council until she died, and leave her position to Duyong's daughter, Wulan. Only water knew why Mother had fixated on me instead of Duyong's chosen successor.

William stirred beside me and I held my breath, hoping, though I knew I shouldn't.

Warm lips pressed against mine. "I love you, lass. I'll see you aboard the *Islander* tonight. And see that your nightdress stays in your trunk." I gasped as his mouth dropped to my breast, but the tingling kiss to my nipple was over far too soon. Timber creaked and William levered himself out of bed. Within a few minutes, he was gone.

I snorted in the pre-dawn light. My nightdress hadn't left my trunk since I arrived on the island and it could stay there and rot for all I cared. I wanted nothing between William and I tonight.

Thirty

Anne watched as I carefully prodded the white ball, which rolled smoothly across the felt to the black one. A soft click marked the transfer of momentum from one ball to the other and the black glided into the side pocket. Her shoulders slumped in defeat. "All right, you win. Third game in a row. It's as though you've enchanted the balls. They do everything you want them to and gang up on me." She set her billiard cue in the rack.

Even I laughed at that. I could enchant every living creature on land or sea with a song, but these pieces of ivory were beyond my influence. Just like in tennis, it was a matter of angles and force and skill, carefully calculated and acted upon. "Perhaps you should use the time I'm away to practice, so you can beat me on my return," I said lightly.

"I might just do that," she returned, glancing up at the clock. "I suppose I should see you safely on your ship before I take the long, lonely walk home. Perhaps I should pop in and take tea at the White House, for the ladies there will be my only source of female company."

She was taunting me, I knew, for I'd done precisely that one afternoon when Anne had turned up her nose at a Cocos-style confection Cook had made for me with coconut and rice. The prostitutes worked late into the night, but until the coolies finished work for the day, they were free to amuse themselves. And when I'd turned up with a tureen full of Cook's cold, sweet treat to share, I'd discovered that a couple of them spoke passable English…and that they could tell me things about pleasing men that weren't written in any book – no, not even the *Kama Sutra*.

I couldn't imagine Anne and her husband engaged in any pleasurable bedroom activity – I still remembered the day we met, when she'd described sex as the relief of a man's needs, which took only a few minutes. I'd had a few minutes this morning, and it wasn't anywhere near enough. My anticipation had been building all day for tonight. No, for weeks.

"Did they give you some advice for your honeymoon? Is that why you did it?" Anne asked, as if she'd guessed my thoughts.

I'd done it because I knew they'd enjoy Cook's creation as much as I did, but Anne wouldn't understand that. "They did offer advice," I said cautiously, feeling my cheeks heat up.

She smiled knowingly. "Then I had best get

you aboard your ship. You might want to take an afternoon lie-down, because a husband expects a lot of his wife on their honeymoon."

"Honeymoon?" It was the second time she'd used the unfamiliar word. "I'm sorry, I don't understand."

"Ah, I'm sure Mr McGregor will explain to you what one does on a honeymoon. It's customary for a couple who are just married to take some time together to grow used to one another. Very…closely." Her cheeks turned a faint shade of pink.

It was on the tip of my tongue to tell her that I knew William quite well already, so we'd be using the trip to have sex as frequently as possible, but I contented myself with a smile instead.

As we left the Club, I heard men's voices floating out of the window. Captain Hughes, the District Officer and the pilot, I thought, quickening my steps. The last time I'd met Captain Hughes, he'd told me there was no passage available on his ship, but I'd stowed away anyway. William knew what I'd done, but Captain Hughes did not. Everyone on the island believed I'd arrived on the *Islander* and the captain had no memory of carrying me as a passenger, so I hoped to be well away from the island before my story came apart. Away, and with William to defend me.

Anne accompanied me aboard without hesitation, giving me a guided tour of the vessel as if she'd forgotten that I'd travelled on it before. A quick search of the cabins revealed William's and my trunks were already stowed in a well-appointed double cabin that had been crammed with supplies on my last trip.

I wouldn't be sleeping with rats this time.

Anne ran her hand over the corner table, then the tops of the two cane chairs arranged around it. "I wish I was going with you. But with Alan going to school in Scotland next year, I don't want to miss any more time with him. Children grow up so fast…" She sighed, then smiled. "I'm sure you'll find that out soon enough. If Mr McGregor wants children, he'd best make himself useful during your honeymoon. You'd best remember, too, that the only way you'll get children is if you…if he…" Anne's discomfiture told me she was never going to finish her sentence.

"If we share a bed at night?" I suggested, nodding at the single bunks placed on either side of the cabin. "It looks like a tight squeeze. When we're under way, I'll ask the cabin staff to help me move them closer together." This didn't seem to alleviate her distress and I realised her real concern wasn't about herself or her children at all. "I'll be fine, Anne. William and I shared a cabin on a cargo ship once and I'm looking forward to revisiting that memory. In these far more luxurious surroundings."

For a moment, she looked shocked and I wanted to take my words back, but she dropped her voice to whisper, "Jackson and I…well, I did tell you I was a nurse during the Great War. What I didn't say is that…sometimes the hospital beds were used by more than just the patients." She blushed.

Before I could ask her for details, she hurried out of the room, wishing me a safe voyage.

Yes. Yes, I wished for a safe voyage, too. One where I didn't have to save William from any shipwrecks or sharks. Sighing, I settled down in a chair, book in hand, to wait for William to join me so our honeymoon could truly start.

Thirty One

Some time during the afternoon, I'd shifted my chair to a better position to watch the comings and goings on the triangular jetty through the window. Yes, window – no poky portholes here, but an unimpeded view through a full-sized window. And a private bathroom, so there'd be no naked sprints along the corridors between my room and the washing facilities. This time, I hoped to avoid the hold altogether.

Captain Hughes returned to the ship, as did most of the crew. Very little cargo was loaded onto the *Islander* – either it was already aboard, or the ship was carrying a very light load back to Singapore. I resolved to ask William when he arrived, but there was no sign of him yet. I wasn't worried – he'd promised to come when he'd finished work for the day and the train trucks were still bumping down the incline from Drumsite. Surely he wouldn't be much longer.

My stomach rumbled threateningly, as it had done several times this afternoon. Perhaps if I sought out something to eat while I waited for William, it might help the time pass more quickly. Water knew I wasn't a patient woman. I slipped on my shoes and strolled confidently to the kitchen.

Déjà vu. That's the phrase I'd heard Anne use when our unvaried activities seemed repetitive. She'd used the words twice this afternoon – each time I inevitably beat her at billiards. My past experience in this kitchen predated my friendship with Anne, though.

For a moment, I recalled the taste of the chocolate cake I'd stolen on my first foray into this kitchen. Now, I'd take William's cake with equal impunity…but I'd leave some to share with him later. Doubting I'd be lucky enough to find such a treat in the kitchen today, I crossed to the room where the refrigerators whirred.

A thorough search revealed neither chocolate or cake, but I did find a pan of kampung fried rice that was more than adequate for my needs. I carried it to the kitchen, where the stove flummoxed me entirely. There was no wood in the kitchen and the stove had nowhere that looked like a firebox. How in water could I heat something up with no fire or wood? Annoyed, I returned the rice to the refrigerator and dug out the fixings for a sandwich instead.

As I placed the second slice of bread on top, I marvelled that this was the first time since I'd left the *Islander* that I'd prepared my own food, for Cook hadn't even let me boil water in her domain. I lifted the sandwich and bit into it, resolving to get a little more practice in the kitchen when we returned to the island. If I'd been paying more attention, I'd have realised that the bread was three days stale and I'd done a poor job of spreading the cold-hardened butter over its crumbly surface.

What I'd give for a cup of tea to wash it down with, I thought, looking around, but the stove still mystified me.

"Ma'am?"

I whirled and came face to face with a man who looked more shocked than I was. I fought the urge to run, as I would have on my first trip on the *Islander*. This time I was a paying passenger, or at least I presumed so, so I stood my ground.

"What are you doing here?" he continued.

I fought to swallow my dry mouthful. "Making a sandwich and wondering what one has to do on this ship to get a cup of tea."

"I can make you tea, ma'am. Would you like

it served in the passengers' lounge?"

There was a lounge on the ship? That was news to me. I'd thought everyone ate in the mess hall outside the kitchen, as they had on the *Trevessa*.

"No," I said finally. "In my room, please." I didn't want William to have to look for me and the first thing he'd do when he came aboard would be to wash and change his clothes.

"Which room, ma'am?"

I hadn't paid attention to the markings on the room door. "Mr McGregor's." Everyone knew William, surely.

His eyes widened. "You're Mr McGregor's sister?"

For a moment, I felt like there was a school of small fish swimming in my stomach. Why did everyone seem frightened at the prospect of meeting Sarah? Should I be scared of the woman, too?

"No. I'm his wife."

Bile rose in my throat and I grabbed my sandwich before striding out of the kitchen. I made it to my cabin before I threw up spectacularly in the wash basin. Thank water for private bathrooms.

Thirty Two

I'd barely managed to tidy myself up and resume my seat in the cane chair when I heard a light, persistent tapping at the door.

"Yes?" I called.

"Your tea, Mem," a Malay voice replied. "I need to get back. The *Yeiryo Maru* needs our berth and Captain Hughes wants all hands to get us ready to leave the cove."

"Come in then."

The crewman cracked open the door and shouldered his way in. I realised why when he set the tea tray on the table before me – the ship's cook hadn't just made tea. He'd produced biscuits and finger sandwiches, then laid them out like a formal afternoon tea for two. I knew I certainly couldn't eat it all.

Hoping the bountiful food meant William was on his way, I thanked the man and he hurried off. I glanced out the window, but it was now too dark to see the jetty, so I gave up and turned back to the table. My sandwich made me sick to my stomach again at the sight of it, but I thought the biscuits should be safe enough. I nibbled on the edge of one, discovered it was shortbread, and began munching happily. Two biscuits later, I decided I needed some tea.

Steam swirled up as I filled my cup and I inhaled eagerly. I shouldn't have – the tea was William's muddy English sort, not the fragrant jasmine I preferred. My stomach clenched in protest.

Oh no. No, not again.

I brought the biscuits back up into the wash basin, along with the water I'd drunk earlier to soothe my bile-burned throat. I splashed water on my face in an effort to freshen up, but I managed to splash the front of my dress, too, soaking through my brassiere to my skin. Clumsily, I shed my wet clothes and climbed into bed, where I drifted into slumber.

I woke to the bass vibration of the *Islander*'s engine in the bowels of the ship. We were leaving, that's all, I told myself muzzily. That's why I was aboard the ship. Because it was taking William and I to Singapore.

William…where was William? I peered around the darkened cabin, but the other bed was empty. No. We couldn't leave without William. If he wasn't aboard, then I needed to return to shore.

I scrambled out of bed, staggering across the cabin as the ship moved beneath me. The wave of dizziness that rolled over me didn't help. Should never have eaten that sandwich.

Those biscuits. Or so much as touched that damn tea…

I barely made it to the wash basin before I fell to my knees, bringing up the remaining contents of my stomach and what felt like the rest of my digestive tract, too. I stuck my mouth under the tap to rinse it, unable to reach a cup from my kneeling position. Then I slumped to the floor and passed out.

Some time later, I woke up enough to realise that I lay on the most uncomfortable bed I'd ever known. Not even Dubhan's stone alcove below the Grotto had been this hard. But my heartbeat galloped along like William's Triumph engine, dragging my senses into alertness. Something else was wrong.

I surveyed the room, but nothing seemed different. Then a chink of light appeared that should have been blocked by the closed door, widening as I watched. A large shadow outside became visible, before it slipped quietly into the room. A sharp click sounded and the room flooded with light, blinding me.

"What are you doing, lying naked on the floor, lass?"

"William," I said weakly, squinting up at him. "Wasn't…feeling well."

"Well, I did plan on carrying you off to bed." His arms encircled me, cold and damp and smelling of the sea, before I sank into a soft mattress. "And I'll be joining you, too. Rowing a lighter from Waterfall after a full day's work is a fool's errand, but when I knew I had you waiting for me…I'd have swum the distance, I swear. We can start our honeymoon in the morning, after a good night's rest."

I settled into my bed. Nothing was wrong now. William was here and everything would be wonderful.

Thirty Three

Weak sunlight tickled my eyelids and I blinked. Filtered through the net curtains, the rising sun seemed gentler. Despite the heat, I cuddled closer to the warm body at my side. It's not often I got to enjoy William at dawn. He'd thrown the bedclothes off, leaving his full, naked glory to be kissed by the morning sun. And me. Definitely by me. Sweat already glistened on his skin, and I longed to lick it off.

There was one part of him I wanted to taste more than the rest. I glanced down and was gratified to see that this bit was definitely awake, even if his eyes were still closed. My thoughts strayed to the *Kama Sutra* I'd been reading last night, describing in infinite detail how to pleasure a man with my mouth, all the while saying that a woman who did that was wanton and not worth sleeping with. Ah, but William would make up his own mind. If he wasn't interested, I'm sure he could suggest another style of sex.

I slid down the bed so I was level with his hips. Leaning over, I pressed a light kiss on the tip, feeling him harden further in response. My loins ached, but I wanted this more. I opened my mouth, then realised I'd need to open it wider still – William was hardly a small man. Feeling like a very nervous whale shark, I grasped his shaft with both hands and guided him between my parted lips. My mouth was full with just the tip. I sucked on him gently, hearing him moan as his eyes flew open.

For a moment, we regarded each other – me with my mouth full of his hot, hard flesh, as his hands curved around the back of my head.

"I'm all yours, lass. If you like the taste of me, take as much as you like."

I took this as permission, swirling my tongue around his salty tip before sucking the length of him down my throat. I'd swallowed fish whole that were a similar size, but never so hot or thrumming with William's pounding pulse. I fell into a rhythm, tasting the length of him up and down as he seemed to swell further until I thought he'd burst.

And burst he did, coating my tongue and throat with salt all the way down. I swallowed, and swallowed again, aware of William's shouts as his hands tugged at my hair, but not wanting to release him until I'd sucked him dry. This was my triumph and I wanted to drink every drop.

He released my hair and I felt him withdraw, until I could press my swollen lips together again. William hoisted me up the bed so that my face was level with his once more.

"That was the best damn wake-up call a man can get," he said. "Were you saving that for the honeymoon?"

"Saving it, yes," I replied. "But I don't know what a honeymoon is, or what we're supposed to do on one."

William chuckled, rocking the bed…no, beds beneath us, for he'd pushed them together while I'd slept. Good. I didn't want to sleep apart and the extra space could come in useful for some of the other things I wanted to try with him.

"Well, normally it's when a husband introduces his wife to intimacy and she adjusts to…"

"Having a hard, pounding penis inside her?" I suggested. I eyed his. "Or having to wait between…um, bouts? Is that the word? Having to wait while he recovers before the pounding can resume? Anne said something about wives having to wait. And she was worried about me. I know I'm not very patient."

William choked. Red-faced, he managed to say, "I was going to say sharing a bed with him."

"I already share your bed," I grumbled. "And I wake up beside you only to hear that your tea is ready or you have to leave for work, without a chance to enjoy our time together before we get interrupted."

William pulled me closer, kissing the top of my head. "I've told the captain and crew not to bother us on pain of…my displeasure. This is our honeymoon."

I perked up. "You mean that it's like our first morning together, and you'll give me more than a goodbye kiss?"

He chuckled again. "After your morning wake-up kiss, I'm about ready to give you anything you want for the rest of the trip, lass. Just name it and it's yours."

"You. Deep inside me for as long as possible and…ohhhh!"

He rolled and entered me swiftly, filling me

with searing heat. "What else do you want, lass?" he asked huskily as he began to move inside me. Deep and then almost out and then oh so deep and…

I let out another moan. "You. You, William. Forever and don't stop…please don't stop "

Thirty Four

Even after a lukewarm bath with William, some of my insides still felt molten. The snarling of my stomach was becoming more and more of a distraction, though, so William insisted that we dress and go to the lounge for breakfast.

I reached for my box of pins as I watched William's reflection buttoning his shirt in the mirror. I wanted those hands on me. My aching breasts, restrained by my brassiere and covered by a modest dress, agreed with me. I set the box down and seized my comb and some ribbon instead. "William, would you braid my hair for me?"

He grinned, took the hair-primping items from my hands and pulled me into his lap on the bed. Fifteen blissful minutes later, his hands cupped my cheeks, turning my head for a kiss. "You look beautiful, lass. I'm going to have trouble keeping my hands off you while we're at breakfast."

"I don't mind," I said lightly.

"I do," he replied, setting his hat on his head. It wasn't the pith helmet he usually wore on Christmas Island. "This is no cargo ship like the *Trevessa*. We'll be in the captain's lounge and on our best behaviour. I wouldn't want to embarrass you, lass."

My heart sank. So much for a holiday – I'd need to remember my high society manners even on the ship. I opened my trunk in search of a hat and gloves.

Suitably dressed, I took William's arm and stepped out into the passage. It was more a veranda than a passage, given that one side was open to the air and sea, even if the waves were several levels below us. If this was as close to the ocean as I'd be able to get, then I'd make the most of it. My life was on land with William and no one would take him from me again.

William had caught my glance at the water. "Don't worry, lass. I won't let anything happen to us aboard this ship. She's new and in good repair, and not a single man aboard would dare cross me. You've nothing to be afraid of."

I laughed – William had misread my mood entirely. "I've never been afraid of the ocean. I was thinking how good it is to be at sea again with you."

William shook his head. "I've never met a man with as much courage as you, let alone a woman. After all that's happened to you…you're remarkable, lass. I'm lucky to have you for a wife."

I gave him a searching look, expecting sexual innuendo in his words, but his admiration seemed to encompass far more than this morning's joining. "I'm lucky you plucked me from the waves, William. I love you." I stretched up to kiss him, but he turned his face away so my lips only met his freshly-shaved cheek.

"Best behaviour, lass. We must both restrain ourselves."

I sighed and we resumed walking.

The captain's lounge was an airy, well-lit room aft of the cabins, but on the same level. The windows faced the ship's wake and the open ocean, for Christmas Island had faded over the horizon some time during the night. Inside, it was furnished with card tables surrounded by cane chairs, and sofas pushed against the walls. It wasn't dissimilar to the lounge at the Christmas Island Club — in fact, some of the sofas were even upholstered with the same fabric. I regretted leaving my Emily Post book behind — I could have done with an etiquette reminder to bolster my resolve, but it was too late now. I'd simply have to brazen it out and use my time in Australia as an excuse for my rusty manners.

William introduced me to the captain with an emotionless: "Mrs McGregor, my wife," and I found myself shaking hands with the man.

Captain Hughes' eyes flared with recognition and my heart sank further. He remembered me from Fremantle. I only hoped some of the stiff manners we were expected to use would stop him from asking how I'd arrived at the island.

William cleared his throat and I dropped Captain Hughes' hand to sit in the chair William had pulled out for me. He rounded the table to sit across from me – tantalisingly out of reach, as if he knew I wouldn't behave myself if I could touch him.

Captain Hughes took the seat between us, marking me as the most important lady present – the only lady present, for there were only the three of us at a table for four – and William as his highest-status guest.

Two servants waited on our table, serving William and I first as if the captain didn't matter. He didn't seem put out by this at all – in fact, his eyes were turned anxiously to William the whole time. I vaguely recalled the captain saying once, long ago in Fremantle, that this was a company ship and subject to the company hierarchy, which placed William higher than him.

Hoping my stomach had recovered from its upset last night, I took a cautious bite of toast. When this didn't seem to cause me too much discomfort, I attempted a little more. After I'd finished it, I decided to try the boiled egg, as the smell of Captain Hughes' was tempting my appetite. I sliced off the top, nodded as one of the servants offered salt, then carefully spooned a tiny portion of egg into my mouth.

"Perhaps Mrs McGregor would like a tour of the ship?" Captain Hughes suggested. "After all, you helped design it for the peculiar conditions it would encounter in and around Christmas Island."

William laughed. "Mrs McGregor doesn't like tours of ships much and she doesn't need to know any more about this one. I'm sure she's already explored it quite thoroughly. More thoroughly than any tour you'd give her, Hughes."

I remembered the tour of the *Trevessa* William had taken me on, and how I'd mistaken the coal-fed boilers for the ship being on fire. I forced myself to keep my eyes on my breakfast and not meet anyone else's. I wouldn't be that silly again.

"Did she help with the design, then?" Captain Hughes asked eagerly. "The passenger cabins, perhaps? I've always had such compliments from female passengers about how well-designed they are. Is Mrs McGregor an experienced world traveller?"

"No," I began, but my voice cracked at the end. I needed a drink. One of the servants saw my distress and came to my rescue with a pot of tea. I nodded gratefully and he poured. Before I could stop him, a liberal splash of milk landed on top.

"My wife stowed away on your ship, Hughes. That's how she got to the island." William's tone turned ominous. "Not a single crewman saw her or thought to mention her to you, either. You should check your ship security if it's so easy for someone to sneak aboard that she managed it."

I swallowed my tea with difficulty, trying not to choke on it. It wasn't Captain Hughes' fault he'd missed a siren on his ship. Hiding from humans came as second nature.

"Yes, Mr McGregor," Captain Hughes said, eyeing me. "Though if Mrs McGregor would care to explain why she chose to stow away aboard my ship…"

"It's not like you gave me much choice," I snapped. "Refusing me passage when I offered to pay for it. What else was I to do when…my…husband…" I trailed off, realising that the tale we'd told the Jacksons relied on my and William's marriage having taken place before the *Islander* left Fremantle. And I'd given Captain Hughes the name Merry had christened me with, not McGregor at all.

Captain Hughes knew too much that contradicted all I'd told the people on the island.

Could I kill him? That was common practice among my kind for humans who knew too much. Perhaps I could…

No. Humans didn't kill each other and I was trying to be human.

I reached for my tea and gulped more down. The taste hit my tongue and I almost retched. William's muddy brew, compounded with a copious quantity of milk. Oh no, not again.

I closed my eyes, fighting to keep my breakfast down. The tea. The damn tea…

"My God, your wife. It must be seasickness. Mrs McGregor, are you all right?"

I pressed my lips together, knowing if I opened them I'd throw up on the table. There had to be another way to maintain his silence without killing him. Perhaps…

"We need smelling salts. Mrs McGregor, do you have smelling salts on you?"

I shook my head.

"In your things? In your cabin?"

I hesitated, then nodded. If I could get Captain Hughes alone, perhaps I could beg for his silence. If he swore he wouldn't speak to anyone about Fremantle or my unconventional trip aboard the *Islander*, then my story was safe. That was the human way, wasn't it?

"I'll go. You keep an eye on my wife." William's tone held dire consequences for anyone who argued.

I waited for him to get far enough out of earshot before I spoke. "Captain Hughes, I need to ask a favour from you. What my husband –"

"I'm sorry, Mrs McGregor," he interrupted. "I'm sorry, but I can't go against your husband's orders. I've told you before, he's higher up than me in the company and if I don't do what he says, I could lose my job. I have a wife and children of my own, so I can't do that. You'll have to take it up with him yourself." He managed a sickly smile. "And if you know the man you married as well as I do, ma'am, you won't argue with him. He has a terrible temper and I'd hate to see a beautiful woman like yourself harmed by Grumpy McGregor."

Could my heart sink any lower? I think it had settled into my left shoe. William had the man so scared that he didn't dare do any favours for me, no matter what they might be. He hadn't even wanted to consider it. But I didn't want to kill him. The ship needed its captain and he did seem like a capable man. Why wasn't there some middle ground between the ways of his people and mine? Killing him seemed so unnecessary.

I felt a resurgence of nausea at the thought. Remembering how it had helped banish my seasickness on the *Trevessa*, I started to hum my mother's lullaby. The one that soothed and it certainly did, easing my nausea just enough to let me open my lips again.

Perhaps I could sing to make him forget, weaving forgetfulness into the melody in the hope that it might be effective. If I could will my desires to other humans through a song, surely it would work on him. I kept the song quiet – barely within the reaches of human hearing – as I concentrated on how much I needed the captain to forget. To forget ever having met me in Fremantle, or William's revelations today.

I didn't stop until I heard William's footsteps returning. "I don't know where they are, so I had to dig some out of the first aid kit." The sharp smell of ammonia reached my nose and I gave an inadvertent sob as it threatened my control over the contents of my stomach. "Right. That's it. I'm taking you back to your cabin."

William's arms lifted me from my seat, holding me tight to his chest as he carried me out. I only hoped my song had done its work on the captain.

Thirty Five

The moment the door closed, William's step lost its certainty. He set me down on the bed as if he thought I'd shatter, but his arms stayed around me. If anything, they tightened instead of letting go.

"What's wrong, lass?" He looked and sounded as if he might cry.

"I don't feel well. The tea. I smelled the tea and it made me ill." I couldn't explain it. I'd never been sick, not once, since I set foot on land. There'd been that first, rum-induced hangover on the *Trevessa*, but nothing since. I'd seen the men in the fish market fall ill when they ate bad food, drank water that had been sitting too long in the rainwater tank or their poor hygiene caught up with them, but never me.

What in the world was messing with my body now?

"We shouldn't have…I shouldn't have…was it what we did this morning?" He stepped back, his arms hanging helplessly at his sides. "Are you feeling sick because you…" He waved at his groin.

I laughed softly. "I was much more ill last night before you were on the ship. Last night what set me off was tea." I eyed his pants. "In bed with you this morning, I felt much better. It's only when I drank tea that I felt unwell again."

William sagged in relief. "I'll take care of you, lass, I swear. What do you want me to do?"

I wanted him to stay with me and never leave me. But confining a man like William to the cabin for the whole trip would be cruel – even I didn't want to stay in bed all trip. Not when I could taste the spray from the ocean if I stood on deck.

"Just having you here with me helps," I admitted. "I don't know what's wrong, so I don't know what else to do. Anne would know, or another nurse. A doctor. A…" I closed my mouth before I finished my last sentence. A healer would know, I would have said, and that meant I should know. Mother had trained as a healer under her mother, and she'd passed this knowledge on to me. How to keep our people alive, producing children, and leading them into the future. Fat lot of good that did me now. I didn't know what would make a mermaid vomit at the smell of tea so suddenly, when it hadn't affected me this way before.

"I'm sorry I'm an engineer, then, lass. I can

fix an engine or a ship or a railway, but the workings of your body are a mystery to me."

Not all of them, I thought. He knew my body better than I did, coaxing it to levels of ecstasy I hadn't believed possible.

"Would you like me to read to you?" he asked. When I stared, he went on, "It's what Mother made us do when one of the other children was sick. We each took it in turns to read aloud. My brothers usually brought in forbidden stuff so they could blame it on me if they were caught with it. I didn't understand half of it sometimes, but one that I remember was *Arabian Nights*. Rob…or was it Tom? I can't even remember now. One of my older brothers, anyway. He was reading it to me and he'd barely gotten past the beginning about the king's wife, Scheherazade, when Mum came in, clouted him round the ear and told him off for reading a filthy book. For once, it wasn't. She sent Sarah in to read to me instead and I told her about the book and the woman who'd dared to save other women's lives with stories.

Sarah…she knew where Mum kept the books she confiscated from my brothers, so she went right out and stole that book back. Mum was much too busy to remember, so Sarah read that book to me instead. All about Sinbad and Aladdin and magic and religions I'd never heard about…we dreamed of adventures we'd go on to see all the places in the book. Now we're all grown up…married, even, and she's at home, taking care of her husband and children. And there's me." He laughed humourlessly. "Living the adventurous life we said we would, among Sikhs and Muslims and Buddhists and who knows what on an island at the ends of the Earth."

"And me," I added quietly. I was the who-knows-what, even if William didn't realise it.

"You are my Bedr-el-Budur, or however you say it. The beautiful princess who I can't resist and don't deserve, but I will risk everything for anyway. And no matter how many times fate tries to take you from me, I will fight for you one more time." He chuckled at my blank look. "I still have the book, but I didn't think to bring it with me. I'll have to write to Sarah and ask her to send it. When it arrives, you're welcome to read it. Or I'll read it to you, if you like, lass, as Sarah did to me."

"You mean if I'm still not well when we get home?" The words left my lips before I realised it. And I sounded frightened.

"No matter what state your health is in," William soothed, lifting me into his embrace. "But with luck, this will pass and you'll be right as rain before we reach Singapore. So, what would you like me to read to you, lass?"

I smiled wanly. "None of the books I brought. I've already read them several times and I'd only be listening to the sound of your voice. I'd prefer you tell me a true story. Tales of what you've done while we've been apart, like you used to tell me on the *Trevessa* when I couldn't understand you very well." And you told the water dragon in the Grotto, who was really me in my true form, I thought but didn't say.

"I'll always wonder how much you did understand on the *Trevessa*," William said thoughtfully. "Sometimes, you'd look at me like you understood every word but you just lacked the ability to speak in response. Other times, it was like trying to talk to a coolie fresh off the boat from China. But you listened. Like you were drinking every word in and you wanted more, so I said…damn, I must have talked for hours. I'd have bored you silly if you'd understood." He stretched out on his bed, which one of the crew must have made while we were at breakfast. "All the while, I was wishing you'd tell me your story. How you came to be on that raft, who your husband was before you were cast adrift, the amazing childhood you must have had, growing up in a place just like this…while I was dreaming of a life out here, you were living it."

"Cocos is not like Christmas Island," I objected. "The weather is the same, but the islands are flat and mostly sand, with only a little rock. There are crabs…oh so many crabs…but different ones to here." I sighed. I could tell William about Cocos island life, but it was not my life, for I'd grown up beneath the surface. Coral gardens that rivalled the coffee gardens at Christmas Island, with a kelp hammock swung between for sleep. Shallows where it was safe to birth and raise children, but deep water nearby for the bigger fish we preferred to eat. I shook myself. "My stories can wait for if you're sick in bed, William. Tell me…tell me a tale of what Grumpy McGregor saw when he first arrived at Christmas Island. And your first encounter with a robber crab."

William turned red. "Oh, you don't want to know that, lass. It was quite embarrassing, really."

I smiled. "All the more reason to tell it. Go on, William. It can't be worse than the time one stole your drawers outside the Grotto while we were making love."

"I…well…perhaps I should start with how I got to Christmas Island. I left Singapore on the old *Islander*, the one that's now called the *Moni*, smuggled aboard by the first officer. He'd been told to replace some missing crew members and if I pretended to be one of them, he told me, he'd give me free passage to Christmas Island. I'd have to do my fair share of work on the ship, but seeing as all my things went down with the *Trevessa*, I figured it was a good deal. We'd been at sea for a couple of days and this big, cloudy mass rose out of the sea like some sort of nightmare. I shouted that we'd hit it and be smashed to kindling, but the other men just laughed and said they knew the secrets of navigating the place and we'd be docking there. Five days we drifted offshore, waiting for the swell to calm enough to steam into the cove, but when we did, I fairly leaped off the ship onto the jetty. In all the confusion of unloading, I wasn't missed at first, and I made some enquiries about the mine office and made my way up to meet the manager. It was McMicken then, not Jackson, though Jackson was keeping the accounts here already. McMicken all but hugged me, he was so thrilled to see me. He'd seen the papers and heard on the radio about the *Trevessa* and our trip across the ocean, and he'd been waiting patiently for me to arrive. The whole South Point expansion was waiting on me, you see — a second engineer, so one could take care of South Point, while the other managed the port and Settlement. And then he asked me how I'd enjoyed my cabin on the *Islander*, because he'd kept one reserved for me since I boarded the *Trevessa* in Liverpool. The first officer, who'd known my name and that I was to be an engineer at the island, had robbed me of my board and accommodation, worked me harder than a coolie, and not paid me a penny for it.

"So I asked the manager to point me to my island accommodation, then strolled up to the jetty, where the *Islander* was still unloading. The first officer spotted me and called me some very uncomplimentary names, telling me to get back to work. I folded my arms and refused. The other men found this funny, but they kept unloading. I didn't know then how quickly the swell could roll in, and how every hand was needed, but no matter. The first officer strode up the pier toward me, threatening me with a beating and the loss of a month's pay if I didn't do what I was told."

William grinned lazily, and I already guessed the ending. I'd seen him fight before.

"That was all the invitation I needed. I beat him soundly, for he was a far inferior opponent, so when he fell unconscious to the deck, I left him where he lay. By that time, the captain had come out to find out what was going on, and I told him it was just a wager — the first officer and I had a bet on who would win a bout of fighting. The captain wasn't pleased, but I told him I was leaving the ship here anyway, so there'd be no further trouble. He asked how much the wager had been for, so he could pay his first officer's debt if the man didn't regain consciousness before the ship left port. I said the officer could settle his own debts — he'd know where to find me on the island. And he'd best not seek any further fights with me or any of my men on the island, or his widow would be left wanting."

Widow? Oh, so that explained it.

"First Officer Hughes made captain six years later, but he never forgot his lesson. And he's never put a foot wrong since. Wouldn't want to, either. He knows I'd kill him."

Thirty Six

When morning tea time arrived, my belly ached more from laughing than from illness and William had almost talked himself hoarse, but I sensed he'd barely dipped beneath the surface of the sea of stories he had to tell. And I was fascinated by every one.

"I'm as dry as phosphate dust, lass. Would you mind if I ordered some tea?"

I hesitated. The smell of it in these close

quarters was sure to set me off again.

William seemed to guess my thoughts. "Do you think you could manage to sit out on deck in the open air? I'll have the crew set out some deck chairs at the stern, out of the wind."

Sun, sea, breeze… "No. I want to sit in the bow, where I might be able to taste the spray. And ask…ask if they have any Chinese jasmine tea, or Japanese green. Perhaps that won't unsettle me so much."

He leaned over and kissed my lips lightly. "You stay here and rest while I take care of everything."

I'd been resting for hours and the only thing wrong with me was my unfortunate inability to keep food down, so the moment the door closed behind him I levered myself off the bed and walked cautiously to the mirror. Ill or not, I was sure he still wanted me on my best behaviour, which meant an impeccable appearance. And a hat. I must have left my gloves in the captain's lounge earlier, so I didn't bother with those. They weren't much use on a ship, anyway — so unless William insisted, I resolved to keep my hands bare at least until we arrived in Singapore. That was two or three days away, William had said, and I hoped my illness would fade long before that. My eyes darted to the bed. We had a lot of lost time to make up for.

The door opened behind me. "Are you sure you should be up? I'm happy to carry you all the way down to the deck chairs, lass."

I snorted. "William, I might not be well, but as long as I have legs, I can walk." Thank water my illness hadn't made me lose control of my ability to shift from legs to tail, or William would've been in for a nasty surprise. And I'd have had to sink another ship...

For a moment, he looked like he was going to argue. But I wasn't Captain Hughes and there was no way he'd use violence against me. Nor would I back down. He must have read all of this from my eyes, for the hardness he'd shown outside softened into concern. "You'll…promise me if you feel weak, you'll tell me. Or if you want to return to bed."

Of course I wanted to return to bed with him, but an hour or two's sea air would help to clear my head. I smiled and nodded.

William seized me and kissed me, sudden and sweet and oh so passionate. "I love you, lass."

Before I could reply, he yanked open the door and ushered me out into the passage. Our linked arms were the only parts of our bodies that touched, but he held my heart, tightly twined with his. As the stern-faced man at my side led me down the stairs to the canopy at the bow and the pair of deck chairs placed beside a card table laid with all the accoutrements of a morning tea that would have met with Anne's approval, I knew it was only a façade.

One of the crew helped serve the tea — jasmine for me and the other stuff for William — before retreating to a safe distance. I even caught William's nod to the man, as if he'd ordered him to stand back far enough to keep our conversation private. I could still feel the man's gaze on us, though all he could see of me was the back of my hat.

I glanced at William, trying not to laugh. "So I'm supposed to be on my best behaviour still? I'm not allowed to squeeze in next to you on your deck chair."

His gaze darted to the crew standing aft of us. "As long as they're watching, yes. We're expected to act as cold and distant as any other married couple."

I burst out laughing. "Not words I'd use to describe our relationship at any time, William. You've been nothing but warm since the moment I met you. Oh, except when you thought I was a ghost."

He reddened. "I told you I'm sorry for that. Incredibly, deeply sorry. I wish I could make it up to you. If I'd come to my senses sooner, you might have invited me to tea with your aunt. Is she your only living relative? I remember you saying you had no family."

I thought of mentioning Mother, but she'd

disowned me the day she led the Elder Council to exile me. "Merry wasn't my aunt. Not really. She was just a lonely widow who was kind enough to take me in. Saying I was her niece gave me an acceptable background. Instead of some woman who'd been saved from a shipwreck she had no business being involved in, I was Merry D'Angelo's niece and a respectable widow. I'd still like to introduce you to her one day. You'd have to pretend she was my real aunt, though. I'd ask her to make my favourite chocolate cake – a devil's food cake, she called it, though she'd laugh and say the devil wouldn't be having any, because if he came to call, she wouldn't let him in unless he said please, which would never happen."

William laughed at this, louder than Merry had, though I'd never understood what was funny about it. If Merry could teach good manners to the unruly young mermaid I had been, surely no one else would present anywhere near as much of a challenge.

"Have you thought of where you'd like to

send our children to school? To Scotland like the Jacksons, or somewhere closer? Are there decent schools in Australia?"

I stared at William. "You want…children?" Men didn't care about their children — they were a nuisance that took them away from their work, or so Mother had said. I'd never met my father, only seen him from afar. Living so close to the Jacksons hadn't shown me that they cared any more for their human children, for Anne cared for their son and Jackson seemed to have little contact with the boy.

"Of course I do. I want you to have my children. Boys with your courage and girls with your beauty. They can have something good from me, too, I hope. None of my bad qualities, anyway." William stared out to sea.

Tears sprang to my eyes. William didn't realise the danger posed by any child of mine — a girl like me, indeed. A child who could enslave his people with a simple song. Yet the yearning in his voice was unmistakeable. He wanted her anyway. And I would do anything to give her to him, teaching her to live among humans as I did. Not killing them, not hating them, and perhaps even one day finding love among them. My voice wavered as I said, "I…I would want our children to have your kindness and strength. And your good judgement in when to use it. And…your sense of honour, too, in doing what is right. Defending those who…haven't earned it, maybe even don't deserve it, but who need your help."

"You make me sound better than I am, lass. I don't know that I'm all those things, but it would be good for our children to be. They'd be like one of my ancestors, or at least I think he was. Raibeart Ruadh was a McGregor and my oldest brother, my father and my grandfather were all named after him. There were even books written about his life — though they called him Rob Roy. Probably couldn't pronounce his name properly. They didn't know the half of it, though." William took a gulp from his teacup. "Are you feeling all right, lass?"

He'd evidently noticed that I hadn't touched my tea. I sighed and reached for the cup. At least if I needed to throw up it was only a few steps to the railing and nothing but ocean below. I inhaled and then cautiously sipped. My stomach didn't immediately rebel, so I kept the cup in my hand. "Better," I admitted. Then, to divert his attention from me, I added, "Will you tell me about your ancestor? This…Robert?"

"There's a lot to tell, lass. Even if you'd read the books I left in Scotland, I'd be telling you stories for days." He settled back into his deck chair.

"I don't mind. I love the sound of your voice." I glanced around, wondering if the crewmen had heard me. I couldn't tell from their impassive faces. But this was surely the sort of thing I wasn't supposed to say in public.

"They can't hear you, lass. But I did and I'd give you anything to make you happy. So if it's

Rob Roy you want, it's Rob Roy you'll get!"
I laughed softly, but most of all, I listened.

259

Thirty Seven

A light tap at the door sounded unusually loud in the absence of engine vibration. "Mr McGregor, we've docked in Singapore Harbour. Johnston's Pier. You can disembark at your leisure." Footsteps faded away along the passage.

I untwined my legs from around William's. "Time to get up, then."

William only held me tighter. "There's no

hurry, lass. The *Islander* will be here a week, refuelling and loading supplies. Normally I'd lie abed another hour at least when the ship docks before dawn."

"Only an hour?" I murmured, laying a line of kisses across his chest. "We'd best get started, then."

Being the attentive lover he was, William's hour turned into two and the sun was well above the horizon by the time I pinned my hat firmly to my hair. My cheeks were more than a little flushed, but there was nothing I could do about that. Perhaps people would attribute it to the humidity and not my husband's ability to take my breath away.

William pressed his lips to the back of my neck and grinned at my reflection over my shoulder as he donned a pith helmet that was the same colour as his creamy suit. "You look beautiful, lass, as always. Even if you weren't ill, I'd have to accompany you everywhere just to make sure no one tries to steal you." His smile seemed forced, but at least he only sounded half-serious. His jealousy of any other man who so much as glanced in my direction had lessened a little over the weeks, it seemed.

"Good," I returned. "This is my first time in Singapore and it looks much bigger than any city I've ever seen before. I think I'd get lost among so many people." I closed the lid on my box of pins. "Shall we go and explore?"

William grabbed my pin box and dropped it into my trunk, followed by everything else I'd left on the dresser. "First, we need to pack, because we'll be leaving the ship for a few days. We have a room reserved at the Adelphi Hotel and I think you'll like it. The bed's much bigger, for a start, and the cook there…ah, you'll see at breakfast."

Over the past three days, we'd learned that tea wasn't to blame for my illness, though the smell did seem to exacerbate the symptoms. Delaying breakfast increased the chances that it would remain in my belly once I'd eaten it, so I did my best to ignore the snarling that had already started in my stomach as we descended the gangplank to shore. My gloved fingers tightened in the crook of William's arm as we set foot on land for the first time in four days.

William led me past the immigration and customs office, pointing to the *Islander*. The man at the office window nodded in response. "Christmas Island is part of the Straits Settlements, though we have our own currency, so there's no need to present our papers," William explained softly. "But if you arrive from Australia, you must remember to get them stamped."

I nodded, not really understanding and too distracted to care. The varied smells from scattered food stalls reminded me of the New Year celebrations in the kampung a fortnight before. My stomach tied itself in knots as I was tempted with satay and rice and fruit and foods even I didn't recognise. William led the way to some Indian men who didn't seem to be selling any food, to my disappointment. Instead, they were moneychangers – the currency here in the Straits Settlements was different to the money in Australia or even Christmas Island. To my horror, I realised that all the Australian pounds, shillings and pence I'd saved were worthless here unless I changed them into Singapore dollars and cents. I watched William change a large quantity of money and tuck it safely into his pocket before he led me away.

"Wait," I said urgently, tugging on his arm. I fumbled for my purse. "I need to change mine, too."

"How much do you have?"

I whispered the sum to William, who nodded and returned to the moneychanger.

"How much to change Australian pounds to dollars?" William demanded.

The grinning moneychanger named a sum that was way too low. They argued back and forth for several minutes before they settled on a much higher price. I rapidly calculated the total in my head and unfastened my purse.

William's hand closed over my purse, holding it shut, as his other hand handed over a quantity of his own money, which was exchanged for three times the number of Singapore dollars the contents of my purse would fetch.

"But William, I…"

He waved me into silence with an urgent look and I subsided, biting down hard on my lip to stop myself from demanding an explanation. The money was pressed into my hands and I tucked it numbly into my purse.

Now I had money for satay, at least. I surveyed the stalls eagerly, wondering which was best, but William tugged on my arm. "We're taking a taxi to the hotel. We'll breakfast there."

I searched the street for the motorcars that I'd known as taxis in Fremantle, or even the horse-drawn cabs that these had replaced, but I saw neither. In fact, there wasn't a horse in sight, though there were some cabs that looked small enough to be harnessed to a pony. If there were any ponies…

William hailed a group of men crouching on the ground beside the cabs and they rose, shouting their prices to be heard above one another. William pointed at a cab and the Malay man who I presume owned it nodded and the rest subsided. If I thought he'd engaged us a vehicle, I was mistaken.

"How much to take my wife and I to the Adelphi Hotel?" William asked.

The man held up his fingers and stated his price. William snorted and named a figure half as large. The cab owner grinned and the bargaining began in earnest.

Some agreement was eventually reached and the man lifted the traces so that the seat was level. William handed me into the seat and then climbed up beside me. The cab was very small, so his thigh pressed warmly against mine. He smiled at me, then nodded to the driver and the man set off at a run, still holding the traces, for all the world as if the Malay man were a racehorse.

"It's all right, lass, you can take your nails out of the rickshaw, which is what they call a Singapore taxi." William patted my knee.

Swallowing, I unclenched my fingers from the side of the cab, where my nails had indeed left indentations in the heat-softened leather.

We were soon in the heart of a bustling city, with plenty of human-drawn taxis like ours in the streets. Motorcars, too, I was pleased to see, and the street vendors were even more abundant than beside the port. I wanted to taste everything.

A Malay man wearing a helmet like William's held up white-gloved hands to direct traffic at a busy intersection of streets. I couldn't seem to turn my head fast enough to see in every direction at once, and I didn't want to miss a thing.

William's arm snaked around my shoulders, pulling me closer until I felt him chuckling. "You look like you've never seen a city before, lass. Don't worry — the taxi drivers know where everything is. All we'll have to do is engage a taxi and they'll take us anywhere you wish to go. Singapore is where you can buy almost anything, for it's one of the busiest ports in the world. I need to visit a motorcycle shop, but the rest of our shopping is up to you."

I tugged my purse into my lap. "About the shopping. I have my own money, William. You gave me far too much. You must let me give some back, or at least give you what I have."

Once again, he shook his head. "No, lass. You're my wife, which means everything I own belongs to you, too. If you want to buy silk dresses and pearls to wear every day, then so be it. The company pays for all our expenses on the island and I've had little else to spend money on. The company even paid for my Triumph, and they'll definitely be paying to have it repaired, seeing as it's the Christmas Island wildlife that damaged it. Buy carpets and linens for the house or a pack of dogs to keep you company when I'm at work. Buy a layette for our first baby, for we're certainly doing enough to start one on this honeymoon of ours, and we'll do plenty more before we return to the island. Or buy books we can read together in the evenings, for I know how much you love them."

Reluctantly, I subsided. I had no desire for half of the things he described, but I understood. He'd promised to take care of me and the money was part of him trying to do precisely that. However, I drew the line at dogs. I had an ocean full of creatures at my command – what in water did I need a pack of yapping, fawning, hairy animals for?

I spotted another man directing traffic from the middle of the road and our taxi driver slowed to a halt. After a few seconds, the signalling man waved us forward, but we didn't move. Our driver turned around in the traces and grinned at us. "Welcome to Adelphi Hotel, sir."

Thirty Eight

William assisted me down from the cab and the impact of my shoes on the paved road was jarring. It felt like a long time since I'd seen roads that weren't graded dirt like those on Christmas Island. I was in the city again, but on a far grander scale than Fremantle.

The Adelphi Hotel soared up three storeys high, all arches and columns like the university back in Perth. These weren't golden brown, though – the Adelphi was white. Striped blinds and tropical plants shaded the interior from the sun and curious onlookers like me, but not for long. William tugged on my arm and drew me inside.

The white marble was cool under my shoes compared to the hot street outside. Electric fans whirred high overhead, stirring the leaves of the potted palms placed around the foyer floor.

"Can I help you, sir?" The English voice startled me. The only man I knew who spoke like that was the District Officer on Christmas Island, and though their linen suits could have come from the same shop as William's, this man was easily twice his age.

"Yes. William McGregor, chief engineer at the Christmas Island Phosphate Company. I have reservations for my wife and I." William's voice had hardened again.

"Christmas Island? Yes, Mr McGregor." The man's face seemed to have a slight sneer to it, as if he felt William was beneath him.

"Do you have any luggage?"

William shrugged. "The ship will send it over, I'm sure. If it doesn't arrive by afternoon, send someone to the *Islander* in the harbour to fetch it."

From the man's shocked look, I understood that William had managed to offend him. "Of course, sir." A wave brought a uniformed Malay man to his side. "Take Mr and Mrs McGregor to the honeymoon suite."

I gave William a startled glance. There was a room dedicated for honeymoons? We followed the uniformed man across the foyer.

"Hughes must have sent word when we docked," William said in a low voice once the Englishman was out of earshot. "A little more ostentatious than I'd like, but you deserve it, and the company is paying, after all."

We proceeded up the stairs, past more marble, palm trees and polished timber, until we reached a set of double doors.

"Your room, sir," the Malay man said, throwing both doors open.

William gestured for me to go first, and I did, but I only managed a few tentative steps into the room before I stopped. It was similar to William's bungalow, but on a much grander scale. The enormous, canopied bed was draped in swathes of mosquito netting, tied to the corner posts. Another set of double doors led to what looked like a private balcony, with its own collection of pot plants and striped blinds. And beside the bed, a closed door that I presumed hid the bathroom. Now we were on dry land, my seasickness would surely vanish and I'd spend far less time in there than I had on the ship. At least, I hoped so.

I glanced in the mirror by the door and realised I was still wearing my hat. I pulled out my hatpins and laid it on the table, wondering if I could unpin my hair, too.

A hesitant knock sounded on the open door and I tore my eyes from my reflection.

A Chinese girl wearing a white apron that covered her dress from chest to knee entered the room carrying a tray. "Tea, Mem?" The tray was thrust at me, steam curling up from the teapot.

I inhaled. My stomach balked. Not again. I bolted for the bathroom.

After I'd brought up several mouthfuls of bile, I slumped to the marble floor in what had indeed proved to be an opulent bathroom. No, I wasn't seasick. This illness was something else.

Through the open doorway, I heard William say, "No, my wife won't be visiting the morning room for breakfast. We'll have breakfast served privately on the balcony here. Every morning. And make sure there's a pot of Chinese jasmine tea."

Thirty Nine

"Will you be all right if I go and run some errands without you?" William asked, perching on the arm of my cane chair. "It's not like the ship – you'll be perfectly safe in the hotel. If you find you're feeling better, there's a lounge and a billiard room downstairs, and morning tea will be served in the dining room, though I hope to return in time to join you for that. The chef is Swiss and he does the most amazing cakes and confections, including several with chocolate." He winked. "I've been wanting to feed you chocolate again for a very long time."

Though I'd only managed to drink one cup of my milkless tea, I was feeling a little better. Wasn't the purpose of this trip for us to spend more time together? "Where are you going?"

"The motorcycle shop for some parts to fix my Triumph. Perhaps a few spares, too, in case the crabs decide to attack again."

No, the siren will behave in future and not rile them up again, I thought but didn't say. "Can I come with you?" I asked instead. "In Fremantle, I always eyed off the motorcycles, wishing I had the money to buy one, but I was saving for the search for you. Now I've found you, I have the funds to buy what I want. A Triumph like yours." I remembered his generous gift this morning. "I still have enough in Australian pounds."

"Are you sure you want to be riding a motorcycle, what with your state of health and all? You've only had one lesson, lass — you don't even know how to ride all that well yet. Wouldn't you like to wait until you recover and you know what you're doing?" His eyes searched mine and I know he saw the yearning there. No, I didn't want to wait. Patience was a virtue I didn't own and I'd waited long enough.

I sighed. "I want you to teach me and it might be easier if you can show me and I copy what you do on my own motorcycle. But I can wait a few more days, until I'm over my seasickness."

William chuckled. "More like tea sickness. You fall ill from the smell of tea. We leave Singapore early on Saturday. If you're well enough by Friday, I'll take you to buy whatever you wish, provided you promise only to ride with me on the island."

Tea sickness. It was as good a reason as any for my weak stomach. I agreed. William dropped a kiss on top of my head, grabbed his hat and headed out.

I nibbled at the breakfast pastry left on my plate. Buttery, flaky pastry melted on my tongue and I dared to sink my teeth into the soft centre. The bitter taste of chocolate made me gasp in surprise. Had William known the croissant contained chocolate when he set it on my plate? I took another tiny bite and more of the filling came with it. Bitter at first, yes, but it quickly grew sweet and combined with the buttery pastry was definitely something I wanted to eat more of. Provided I could keep it down, of course.

A porter arrived with our luggage, leaving it in the corner of our room before he departed again with our breakfast things and my request for more chocolate croissants for breakfast tomorrow. I unpacked a few things, putting my hatpins in the pin box, then found myself with nothing to do. A burning desire to ask for Merry's advice on my illness sent me back to my trunk for my fountain pen and some writing paper. I could ask her – I just wouldn't get an immediate answer.

I carried my writing things to the desk, only to discover a sheaf of far superior paper already waited there for me. Sheets stamped with the likeness and address of the Adelphi Hotel. I sat down, pulled one of the pretty sheets toward me, and began to write.

I thanked her for her advice and hoped she was well. I told her that I'd found William and that I'd become his wife. I made no mention of my journey to the island or my hermit's life in the cave — that touched too close to the nature I wished to conceal. I described island life, and wildlife, smiling as I wrote about the bat that splattered into my soup at my first dinner on Christmas Island. I explained that I was visiting Singapore on a shopping expedition and then I stopped. I longed to tell her about my health, but everything else I'd written was so cheerful. Did I truly need to trouble her further with my mysterious sea sickness? If I simply avoided the stuff, perhaps my nausea would disappear, too. Maybe…maybe I could ask her in my next letter, I decided, signing my new name for the first time. Mrs Maria McGregor — yes, that was me. Merry would be happy for me, I was certain of it.

The desk held envelopes as well as writing paper, so I sealed my letter in one of those, carefully addressing it to Merry. I turned it over to write my return address and faltered, because I wasn't sure how to address a letter to Christmas Island as I'd never received one before.

A crash made me jump. I stared at the open door, which the porter had definitely closed behind him. William looked almost as surprised as I was.

"Sorry, I'm late, lass," he said breathlessly. "Didn't have all the parts I wanted. Some will have to be ordered from the factory and that'll take weeks." He slumped against the door frame, panting as if he'd run all the way up the stairs before he crashed through the door. "What did you do while I was gone?"

I waved at the envelope. "Writing a letter to Merry in Fremantle. I wasn't sure what our address was for her to reply to."

"Just care of the Christmas Island post office, lass. In the Straits Settlements. It'll reach you."

I scribbled as he spoke. "Thank you. Is there a post office here in Singapore where I can post it?"

"Of course, lass. I'll take it for you unless you're feeling well enough to venture out to do some shopping with me this afternoon." He grinned. "After our conversation this morning, I can't get the thought out of my head of how much I'd like to see you in silk." His eyes strayed to the bed. Sure enough, the bedspread looked like it was made of a shiny fabric that could be silk.

"Whatever you have planned sounds wonderful to me," I replied, reaching for my hat. "But first, you promised me Swiss chocolate."

Forty

The week whirled by in a riot of activity. Shopping, tasting the delights of the mysterious chef's tea and cakes, more shopping, seeing the sights, more shopping and dinner, then falling into bed and William's willing arms for the climax of my day. Well, given that my lover was William, usually several. He was unfailingly generous and I didn't stint him, either. I'd never felt so well-loved in my life.

My trunks had multiplied from the half-filled one I'd brought from Fremantle to four, all packed to the brim. I had enough dresses to last me a month without washing, and riding pants just like William's, though tailored to fit my curved body. We'd found a tea merchant who had both Chinese jasmine and Japanese green tea, so several chests of the stuff had been sent to the *Islander*. One trunk was filled with books alone, to my delight and William's amusement. I opened it just to stare at all of my new treasures, anticipating the pleasure of reading them on the veranda at home while I waited for William to return for breakfast.

"Don't forget this one." William held up the volume from my nightstand.

"I haven't. That belongs to the hotel. I should return it before I forget." I took the book from his hand and headed downstairs to the hotel library. At the foot of the stairs, I almost ran into a boy dressed in the hotel uniform.

"A message, Mem," he said, holding out an envelope.

I scanned the front. It was similar stationery to the envelope I'd posted Merry's letter in, only this had a different hotel name stamped on it: the Raffles Hotel. A rival but inferior establishment to the Adelphi, or so William had said. "This is addressed to my husband. He's in our room upstairs. You'd best take it to him."

The boy nodded and raced up the stairs.

Out in the courtyard, the caged parrots started up a cacophony that probably meant a stray cat had entered the yard. Some people pitied the birds their cages, instead of letting them fly free, but their prison bars meant security and protection. They were fed by hand, cosseted by countless guests and even now a boy ran out with a stick to chase the cat away.

I continued on to the library, returned my book to the shelf with a longing look at its companions and the comfortable reading room, before reluctantly heading back up to our room. The boy was nowhere in sight and William had his hat in his hands.

"We're invited to tea at the Raffles this afternoon, lass, before the *Islander* departs," William told me. "So make sure everything's packed, for we won't be coming back here this trip."

All my things were already packed, so I shrugged. "Who do we know who'd stay at the Raffles Hotel?"

William smiled thinly. "Hughes always stays there. And so do other Europeans who've read Kipling and know nothing of Singapore. When there are new passengers for the *Islander*, though, Hughes invites everyone to afternoon tea to get acquainted. He's well acquainted with me and he's already met you, so I presume Mr Murray has finally come to visit the island to inspect the mine. He's been absent nigh on ten years, they say, so he's overdue for an inspection. He'll stay in Edinburgh, in the original European houses in the cove, but expect a full round of society engagements if he brings his wife or his daughter."

Good thing I'd been practicing my etiquette day and night here in the hotel. I hadn't noticed a single pitying glance pointed toward me in my time here — something I'd never managed during an afternoon tea with Anne.

"Shall we, then?" I asked.

Forty One

Our rickshaw pulled up outside a grander building than the Adelphi appeared to be, if only because the Raffles Hotel wasn't wedged in between buildings of a similar size. This grand edifice stood alone. A pity, though, for its isolation meant there was no shelter from the torrential afternoon shower other than in the hotel itself. William hoisted an umbrella above us to keep the worst of the rain off me as we ran for the entrance.

Inside, I saw little difference to the Adelphi aside from the layout. The opulence I'd become accustomed to didn't faze me in the slightest now, though the marble floors were decidedly slippery under my rain-slicked shoes. I grasped William's arm firmly and managed not to lose my footing today, though I had an interesting collection of yellowing bruises from colliding with palm trees as I slipped and slid on the wet marble at the Adelphi after the daily afternoon downpour.

One of the hotel staff took William's hat and umbrella and I was tempted to hand him my hat, too, just to see what he did with it. It was firmly pinned to my hair, though, so I resisted temptation. If we were meeting William's employer, I needed to look my best.

We entered a crowded dining room and William paused in the doorway to search the faces of those present. I spotted Captain Hughes almost immediately, seated beside a woman with her back to me. His gaze met mine and he rose, offering a slight bow in my direction. The woman turned in her seat to see what had caught her companion's attention. Ocean blue eyes set in a pale face mesmerised me, just as they had the first time I'd seen them. William pulled me aside to allow the passage of one of the hotel staff, bearing a laden tray of steaming teapots. Steam wafted behind him, clouding the air as I inhaled. And my stomach revolted.

I dropped to my knees and decorated a potted palm tree with the regurgitated remains of my lunch. Inwardly, I cursed the waiter and all tea-drinking Englishmen to oblivion. For a moment, I wanted to raise my voice in a song to change their taste for tea forever. But humans didn't enslave the minds of other humans, I reminded myself. Especially not when one of them had those unmistakeable eyes.

A strong hand grasped mine and helped me to my feet.

"Thank you," I said, turning to smile at

William.

"You're welcome, lass," said the woman who was unmistakably his sister.

Beside her, William coughed. "Ah, this is my wife, Maria, and this is my sister, Mrs Whyte."

"Sarah," she corrected, eyeing me up and down. "Good thing I'm here, Will. I had a feeling I was needed when I didn't hear from you. I didn't think it was because…well, congratulations." She turned to me. "How did he take the news?"

"What news?" I asked hoarsely.

Sarah glanced from me to William, then elbowed me painfully in the ribs.

I whimpered and pushed her away.

She nodded knowingly. "Is that tender, lass? Don't know what your mother was thinking, not telling you what to watch out for."

My mother told me to watch out for plenty. Nosy, interfering humans for a start. But William would never forgive me if I killed his sister. Who'd probably faint if she knew what my mother was, let alone her thoughts.

William looked just as lost as I was. Ah, good. Then his sister probably was talking nonsense. I relaxed a little and tucked my arm into his.

"You're going to be a father, you dolt. The lass has morning sickness and all the symptoms of a bonny baby growing inside. I'd best send a note to my husband and tell him that I won't be home for a bit longer. I wouldn't miss being the midwife at this birth!"

My mouth didn't seem to want to close. Tea sickness was the mysterious mother's malady and my exile was over. If I chose, I could return to my people. And leave William.

No. Never. I was one bird who'd never fly away from those I loved. I'd close the door of my cage and lock it. This time, I would throw away the key.

Forty Two

Sarah insisted that we share a taxi to the *Islander* after we'd finished our afternoon tea and I immediately agreed, despite William's worried look. I wasn't sure what he was worried about, either. He handed me and then Sarah up into the cab, saying, "I'll be right behind you," and pointing to his own rickshaw, whose driver waited patiently.

Once we were underway, Sarah began to ply

me with questions. How far along was I, when had my illness first started, what was I planning on naming the child, when did I plan to visit Scotland… After my answers devolved into a string of "I don't know," "I'm not sure," and "I'll have to discuss that with William," she began telling me about all the delights of pregnancy I had to look forward to, as well as the birth. Her face grew increasingly animated as she related the details of a particularly difficult birth she'd assisted with back in Scotland. Fortunately, we arrived at the pier before she could launch into another gruesome tale.

"Are you all right, lass? Not feeling ill again?" William asked anxiously as he helped me out of the cab. "You're looking a bit pale."

I assured him I was fine, but I don't think he heard.

He didn't leave my side as the crew made ready for the *Islander*'s departure. The sun set in a magnificent blaze of colour as we pulled away from the pier, but William and Sarah didn't seem to notice. They conversed in low voices that were almost drowned out by the rumble of the engine so that even I couldn't discern the words. Frequent glances in my direction told me I was definitely the topic under discussion, though.

When the ship left the harbour and the lights of Singapore grew further away, William pulled me into their little family conference. "I'd like Sarah to examine you," he said. "And the…baby. You and the baby."

I wanted to refuse, but I knew I'd need someone to assist with the birth. I didn't trust a mermaid midwife with my child, so I'd have to rely on a human one. "Very well."

"Right now," William insisted, tugging me away from the rail.

When he closed the cabin door behind Sarah, my nervous anticipation grew. Human midwives didn't use dolphins in their examinations, so this would be my first taste of human medical practice.

I was required to undress and then poked,

prodded, listened to and measured as I squirmed under Sarah's probing fingers. William watched impassively, but the shadow in his eyes and the nervous bobbing of his Adam's apple as he swallowed frequently told me he was worried. Whether about me, the baby or our family situation, I didn't know, and he didn't say.

After a while, Sarah finally permitted me to dress, but she disappeared into our bathroom to wash her hands without speaking about her findings.

It wasn't until she'd dried her hands that she returned to the cabin and perched on one of the cane chairs.

"Well?" William demanded. "Is she or isn't she?"

"God preserve us from first-time fathers," Sarah responded, glaring at him. "Yes, your wife is pregnant, Will. About eight or nine weeks, I'd say, based on the size of her belly. Everything seems in order and they're both healthy enough."

"But…the sickness?"

She sighed loudly. "Normal. Perfectly normal. In my experience, the more sickness a mother has, the healthier the baby is when it's born. As long as she eats enough and gets a bit of exercise every day, come September, you'll be holding your first child in your arms."

William's breath hissed out in relief.

"Now, I'm told we have to dress for dinner and the captain's expecting us, so if you'll excuse me, Will, apparently my afternoon tea clothes aren't good enough to be worn to a fancy dinner, so I need to get changed."

"Tell Hughes we won't be joining you. I'll send for some sandwiches from the galley if we get hungry," William replied, his eyes on me. Did I detect a dangerous glitter in them, or had I imagined it?

The door clicked shut behind Sarah. William seized me in a fierce embrace, crushing his lips against mine. My desire flared in response and I left off trying to fasten my brassiere. Instead, I wrapped my arms around William and returned his passionate kiss. This seemed to set his ardour ablaze and he turned us around, pushing me toward the bed. Unused to the crowded cabin, I edged around one trunk only to catch my foot on the corner of another. I fell heavily against one of the cane chairs, tipping it over as I continued my descent to the deck.

"Are you all right?" William gasped, reaching for me.

"Fine," I mumbled, wincing as I surveyed my body for what felt like a dozen forming bruises. My breasts had spilled out of my brassiere, too, which now hung halfway down my arms. William pulled it out of the way and threw it aside before he lifted me up and carried me the rest of the way to the bed. Now I was clad in only my drawers, but William didn't leave me those for long. He yanked down the waistband and pressed his lips to my belly. Soft kisses feathered my skin, all the while edging lower.

"Lass, do you think…are you feeling well

enough to…" He laughed softly. "My head feels like I'm flying. I'm going to be a father and you, my beautiful wife, are carrying our child in here." Another kiss. "To blazes with propriety. I want you. God, you don't know how much."

If he could feel the intense desire that had plagued me for weeks, he wouldn't say that. "Not as much as I want you, William."

He stripped off his clothes, throwing them on the floor as if he didn't care where they fell. Now as naked as I was, he surveyed my body as if he couldn't decide what he wanted to do first. "Is there anything we shouldn't do, you know, because of the baby?"

I pulled him down to the bed on top of me. "As long as you don't stop, everything will be fine, William." I whispered, arching my back as he plunged his fingers inside me. "Please don't stop."

Forty Three

The next morning at breakfast, Sarah glowered at William and wouldn't say a word beyond her first curt, "Good morning." My body ached for more of William's touch, but we sat across from each other in the captain's lounge, behaving like a proper, polite married couple. Even if my thoughts strayed more than once to the thrill of William taking me on the table, beside the bowl of raspberry jam, I made sure my expression didn't betray me. My cup of Japanese green tea was never far from my lips, blocking out the smell of anyone else's tea.

As before, our deck chairs were arranged under the canopy at the bow, but with the addition of a third for Sarah. It remained empty, though, as William produced our new-found copy of *Arabian Nights* and proceeded to read it aloud to me.

Sarah's angry footsteps paced the deck from bow to stern to back again, but she didn't even join us when our tea was served. I presumed she took hers with the captain inside, but I didn't pay her much attention. William's storytelling enthralled me far too much for that.

All good books come to an end, and it was toward the end of our afternoon tea that William closed this one. He gulped down the remains of his lukewarm tea and asked, "Would you like another book, lass?"

"Yes, please."

"I'll be back directly, then." He ambled off

toward our cabin.

Only a few seconds passed before Sarah landed in the chair beside me, panting as if she'd been running. "How'd you get that?" She pointed at a darkening bruise on my calf from my encounter with the chair last night.

"I fell," I answered.

She snorted as if she didn't believe me. "I've heard that one before, many times. I bet it's not the only one, is it?" She lifted the hem of my skirt and surveyed the results of a week's worth of clumsiness and slippery floors, which were just a backdrop for yesterday's blooming fresh bruises. "How could he? I never thought Will would…"

I yanked my dress down over my knees. "It's not his fault. It's not like he can control —" the weather, I wanted to say, but she didn't let me finish.

"He bloody well should be able to control himself, at least."

I thought of last night and reddened. Neither of us had been particularly restrained, but William could hardly shoulder more than half the blame for it. My desire had burned at least as brightly as his, if not more so. "It was my fault, honestly. He said…" Propriety made me hesitate. Talking about sex in public was definitely taboo and saying he couldn't control his sexual urges around me would only make him look weak to the crew, when he was nothing of the sort.

"They all say that, too, lass. He's already gotten you pregnant. You've more than done your wifely duty for the moment. He shouldn't be forcing himself on you at night any more. I'll have a word to him, I will." I recognised the grim look on her face — I'd seen it on William's at the start of a fight.

"No, please don't say anything," I begged. A week of sharing William's bed properly again wasn't anywhere near enough. If she said something and he stopped making love to me or even sleeping with me altogether, I wasn't sure I could bear it again.

"So you finally decided to join us," William

said brightly, throwing himself into his deck chair. "What would you prefer, lass? I have a collection of children's stories by Kipling and some dreary sounding one by a woman named Jane Austen. *Pride and Prejudice* or something equally pretentious."

My head was roiling at the prospect of Sarah messing with my relationship with William. As if our life together wasn't challenging enough with…what I was. "I don't mind. Whatever you like, William." My voice came out flat.

William noticed, as he always did. "Are you feeling all right? I can take you back to our cabin if you like, lass. You could have a bit of a lie down before dinner. Unless you'd like to skip dinner altogether? I'll keep you company, of course." He winked.

Sarah glared at him. "I'd never have thought it of you, Will. You were a good man when you left Scotland. What happened out here to turn you bad?"

Before either of us could respond, she rose and stalked away.

William stared at her departing back for a moment before he shook his head and turned back to me. "I didn't think I was being so obvious, but Sarah's been married a while now, even if it is to a man who hides his wedding tackle with underpants under his kilt. She's probably converted him into a proper Scotsman now, so there's no hiding such things from her. Sorry if I embarrassed you, lass."

"No worries." I glanced at the books. "I would like you to read to me some more. It's so nice out here in the breeze. Nothing's as pretentious as Kipling. Let's try the Austen book and see."

William settled into his seat and cracked open the book. "It is a truth universally acknowledged," he read, "that a single man in possession of a good fortune, must be in want of a wife." He grinned. "Well, they got that right. I certainly want you, my beautiful wife." And he read on.

Forty Four

William's passion didn't abate that night, nor the one after, so I assumed Sarah hadn't spoken to him yet and I was very thankful for it. Mine work would steal him soon enough, I knew, for I could already see the misty form of Christmas Island on the horizon. I stayed in the cabin to pack, as we'd been terribly messy with our clothes in the few days we'd been aboard the Islander. I'd found a pair of drawers under the bed and I suspected I'd find more if I managed to crawl under there. Ooh, what if they'd been lost under the bed on our outward voyage and remained here the whole week we'd been in Singapore? While the crew cleaned the room as well!

I smothered a giggle as I dropped to my knees. Would William be jealous of any man who looked at my underwear even when I wasn't wearing it? I crawled under the bedstead.

Several minutes later, I emerged with two pairs of my drawers, one of William's socks and a stocking that I was certain wasn't mine. I brought the haul out onto the veranda to check in the better light. Oh, wait, the stocking was mine after all. It must have fallen from my trunk at some point and I hadn't noticed.

Raised voices drew my attention and I spotted Sarah and William standing beside the railing at the bow. From his folded arms and thunderous expression, I guessed the topic of discussion.

I threw the undergarments into my trunk and hurried down to the foredeck. I could already hear her words as I approached.

"…she's carrying your child, Will. You should be treating her like the fine china she drinks her tea out of, instead of banging her like a drum at Hogmanay. You can't do that to a woman who's with child. Tom or even Rob I'd believe it of, after they'd had too much whisky, but Cat and Beth would've been knocking down Mum's door the next morning, threatening to get the police involved. Mum would've shouted herself hoarse and they'd never do it again. You were always the best of them, Will. Never so much as stole a kiss from a lass back home. And look at you now…that terrified lass you call your wife won't stay with you, you know. And if you hurt her, you'll hurt the child, too. Mum would be ashamed of you, Will, and Dad…if he was still alive, he'd beat you bloody, and rightly so, too."

"Relations between me and my wife are none of your concern, Sarah. Stay out of it."

Sarah was as stubborn as William, I realised with a smile. "But it's not just between you and your wife, Will. I bet everyone on the ship knows what you do to her. Even if they're not in the cabin next to you, they're not deaf. How long do you think it'll be before one of them reports you to the local magistrate?"

"For loving my wife? Sarah, there isn't a man on this ship stupid enough to do that. And those who might be…well, Hughes is the captain here."

"Stupid? No, they're afraid of you, Will. Even Captain Hughes. When I asked him if he knew you were violent, he turned right pale, he did, and said you weren't a man to cross. He said anything you choose to do with your wife is entirely your business and none of his. What's changed about you that terrifies grown men? The devil's gotten to you out here, Will. With your hard hats it seems your head's gotten hard, too. You used to fight to protect girls back home, Will. I remember when James tried to kiss me when we were kids, you bloodied his nose properly and I was grateful for it. But you're not my brother any more. If you truly were my brother, you'd never stoop so low as to beat your own wife."

William stood as open-mouthed as I did. Where in water had she gotten that idea?

Sarah planted her feet firmly on the deck. "I'll stay to take care of the lass until your child is born. Then I'll take her somewhere you can't hurt her any more. And if you even think to lay a finger on her while I'm here…I'll bust your wedding tackle before I report you to the magistrate myself." She stalked off with her head held high.

William stared wordlessly after her. I waited until she'd rounded the corner before I stepped out of my hiding spot. I wanted to hug him and tell him that I'd never leave him, no matter what his sister said, but there were several crewmen in view so I couldn't even touch him.

"You heard?" William asked darkly.

I hesitated, then nodded. "The gist of it, at

least." I wasn't sure what else to say.

"Sarah…" William dropped his voice to a whisper. "Sarah said that I hurt you. That you'd told her so. Is it true?"

I shook my head.

"But you'd tell me if I hurt you, wouldn't you, lass? Even if it was by accident, you'd tell me to stop, right?" he persisted.

I wet my lips. "If it was by accident, I might." His eyes widened in horror. "But if you set out to hurt me deliberately, William, permanent damage to your wedding tackle would be just the start. And I wouldn't bother with a magistrate. You'd definitely need a doctor, William."

He laughed in relief. "There's the lass I love. If I hurt you on purpose, I'd deserve it."

Damn straight he would.

Forty Five

Spinner dolphins surfed the bow wave as we entered Flying Fish Cove. I stood back from the railing, hoping they didn't see me, or if they did, that they didn't recognise me. If they knew about the child I carried, they'd send word to Mother immediately, who'd come to drag me away from my home. Sarah would probably believe her brother had murdered me and thrown my body in the sea, too.

While the *Islander* docked, William pulled me aside. "Can you take my sister up to the house and get her settled in? I need to see to the unloading."

I frowned at him. "Can't work wait until tomorrow?"

"I won't be long. A few hours at most. I promise I'll be home for lunch and dinner, too." He pushed me toward the gangplank where Sarah stood with a bag in her hand.

I sighed. Even if she'd called her brother a wifebeater, I didn't mind the woman. She'd been unfailingly kind to me. Perhaps I could persuade her to listen to reason on the walk up to Rocky Point.

"I'll take you up the house," I offered. Up close, I noticed trepidation in her eyes — the cliffs had looked ominous the first time I'd seen them, too, though I hadn't been looking at the fresh scars of the recent landslide. At least the damaged houses in the kampung had been demolished. Any usable timber was now stacked beside the railway line, presumably awaiting transfer up to South Point. "I can show you around and introduce you to people, if you like."

She nodded and followed me off the ship. I kept an eye on the water below the pier, scrutinising it for signs of nosy dolphins, but their squeaks told me they'd stayed in the deeper water at the entrance to the cove. Good.

Conscious of the contrast between Singapore's busy, paved streets and the muddy track where the only vehicles were our own shod feet, I pointed out what we did have. "The tennis courts are over there on the padang, but you must watch out that the crabs don't steal your ball. The Christmas Island Club is upstairs in that building, above the mine offices. There's a billiard table and a bar, and a room they turn into a cinema when a new film arrives from Singapore." I frowned, remembering the one film I'd watched there. "Don't let Mr Ong choose the film, though. He's overly fond of monsters, I find." The outrigger canoes the Malay men used for fishing sat in a line on the beach, as if ready to head out at any moment. I watched a bosunbird soar overhead and followed its flight with my eyes. I pointed across the cove. "The District Officer's house is on the cliffs over there, but you have to walk the cliff road to get there, so usually we wait for him to come and visit us in the Club. They're usually scared, young Englishmen fresh out of their diplomatic training and they don't stay long. A year at most. The rest of the Europeans are mostly Scottish, like you and your brother. I'm the only Australian." We trudged up the steepest part of the track. The only sounds we made were the squidge of mud underfoot and our panting breath before it was drowned out by the clank of full phosphate cars heading down the incline from Drumsite. "Phosphate from the mines, headed for the drying sheds before a ship comes to pick it up. There was a Japanese ship in when we left, but it's loaded and gone now, so this will be for the next ship."

"What's that?" Sarah pointed at the collection of Chinese grave markers on our right.

I hesitated, wondering how she didn't know. "It's where the Chinese people on the island are buried when they die."

"Oh." She dropped her gaze to stare at her feet. "Graveyards look different in Scotland."

I nodded and turned onto the left-curving track. "Our house is this way, past the Jacksons'."

"That one," Sarah said, pointing. For the first time today, she smiled. "Will sent me photos when it was built. Before that, he lived in the single men's quarters near the port. He said the snoring would shake the walls sometimes."

"I didn't know that," I admitted.

"He wrote me a letter every week without fail. Usually they'd arrive all bunched up together and I'd have to work out the right order to read them in. Sometimes he put in little gifts, like seashells or a feather or some pictures. Once he told me he'd seen a man make a comb out of a turtle shell and he'd send it in his next letter. He never did, though."

"That's because he gave it to me. I had nothing and he…it was the only thing I had with me when the *Trevessa* sank." I pressed my lips together, not wanting to make the offer but knowing I'd have to. "I've kept it safe, if you want it."

Her brow wrinkled. "The *Trevessa*…I know that name. That's the ship Will took from Liverpool. The one that sank and he was drifting at sea for weeks. You were on the ship, too? Have you and Will been married that long without him telling us? But that was years ago and you don't look old enough…" She coughed. "Well, you don't look a day over eighteen. I wish I didn't. No, wait, you can't have been married then or Will wouldn't have been living with the single men."

"William and I ended up in different

lifeboats. His took him to Mauritius, while mine took me to Fremantle, where I stayed with my aunt. Opposite sides of the same ocean and we only found one another again recently. We weren't willing to let fate separate us again." I swallowed. "Sarah, your brother isn't as bad a man as you think. William would never —"

"How was your trip? Did you buy all the dresses in Singapore?" Anne called from her veranda. "Ooh, you should hear the frightening thing that happened here just yesterday. Just wait until I tell you. The Malay fishermen had the most terrifying encounter with a shark while they were fishing. None of them are brave enough to go out in their boats at all after that. They're all lined up on the beach, but no one will go fishing until they know the shark's gone." She made it down the steps before she noticed Sarah. "Oh, I'm sorry. I'm Anne Jackson. My husband is the island manager."

Sarah shook Anne's offered hand. "Mrs

Sarah Whyte. I'm Mrs McGregor's midwife."

Not William's sister. My heart sank.

Anne was too excited by the implications to notice my expression. "Midwife? Do you mean…" She gestured at my midsection.

I managed a smile. "Yes, or so Sarah tells me. I was quite ill in Singapore. At one point, we thought it was the tea making me sick."

"So will you return to Australia to have the baby, or go to McGregor's family in Scotland?" Anne asked. "I had both mine here on the island and I tell you, taking care of a newborn in the tropics is terrible. Even with Amah, I'm not sure how I managed."

"I think Australia sounds far better," Sarah said, her eyes as thoughtful as William's when he was planning something. "Your aunt lives in Fremantle, I'm sure you said only a moment ago."

Give birth to William's baby in Merry's house? And desert William? No, I couldn't do that. I just smiled, though, and let the other two women take over the conversation while I waited for William.

Forty Six

I settled into my reading chair on the veranda, pleasantly full from lunch. My book lay in my lap, but it didn't occupy my full attention. The last of the parts William had ordered in Singapore had arrived and this afternoon his work consisted of repairing his Triumph. In the front yard, right in front of my veranda vantage point.

First, William spread out a large sheet of

canvas beside his motorcycle and laid out the new parts on it, alongside his tools. Next, he started taking the motorcycle apart, matching the damaged parts to their replacements. The warped fuel tank seemed to give him the most trouble, as the crab had not just clawed it open, but it had changed the shape of it so that it caught on things it had no business touching. In the end, when William had unfastened every screw holding it to the frame and it still didn't come free, he took to it with a pair of shears. After several seconds of the teeth-gritting squeal of metal cutting metal, he wrapped both hands around the tank and pulled. With a sucking sound, it popped free…and splattered the sludgy remains of fuel on his white shirt.

William swiftly undid the buttons and removed his shirt, swiping at the black smudges on his well-muscled chest before throwing it on the tarp beside the ruined fuel tank.

I closed my book and sat up straighter.

William grinned as he stripped away the

snipped fuel lines and wires, sweat already forming on his skin from the tropical heat. While he worked, his body took on a decided gleam, as the humidity stopped the sweat from evaporating. I couldn't wait until after dinner, when that gorgeous body would be mine in bed and I could taste the salt glistening on each muscle.

I settled more comfortably in my chair, resting my head on a cushion. Watching William work without his shirt was enough to inspire fantasies far better than those in my book of fairy tales. I must have made some sound, because William winked at me and said, "Do you like what you see, lass?"

I smiled and nodded.

He wiped his hands on his ruined shirt and climbed the steps two at a time until he reached the veranda. William cupped my cheek in one hand and kissed me tenderly. His other hand slipped between the buttons of my dress and caressed my belly. "So do I, lass." A feeble fluttering started under his fingers and I knew the response didn't come from me. William evidently hadn't felt it, though, and he returned to his mechanical work.

I touched my midsection and felt her answering protest. We'd been home two weeks and she'd surely grown in that time, for Sarah measured my belly every week and told me so. Had my first daughter moved at three months? I dredged through my memories, but I couldn't remember. All I remember of that time was being sick with grief at the loss of Giuseppe and the screaming agony of her birth had seemed like a fitting punishment for the woman who'd killed her father. But it wouldn't be like that with William and our daughter. In only six short months, he'd hold her in his arms and we would truly be a family.

And William…William while he was working was mesmerising.

"Maria! Maria!"

I blinked the sleep from my eyes at the sound of my name. Where had the day gone?

"You really shouldn't sleep out here. Didn't

I tell you an hour of bed rest every afternoon?" Sarah demanded.

I shrugged. "You did. But William was…" I waved vaguely in the direction of his motorcycle. Squinting into the sunlight, I realised the Triumph was whole again and the tarpaulin, tools and William were gone, along with my afternoon.

Sarah made an impatient sound in her throat that I knew meant she thought I was crazy. Whether crazy for loving him or something else entirely, I wasn't sure.

"See you tomorrow, ladies," Anne called, heading back to her house.

Sarah and I farewelled her before Sarah started shooing me inside. Tonight's excuse was mosquitoes; yesterday's had been the possibility of catching a cold. As always, I responded that these things didn't bother me, as long as I was there to greet William when he came home.

"You know, there's a black mark on your face. You should go wash up before dinner."

My hand flew to my cheek and sure enough, came away with a faint greasy smudge. I trudged inside. A quick glance in the mirror explained Sarah's bad mood — the black mark was a handprint down one side of my face that looked almost like a bruise. As if William would ever strike me. Dutifully, I took a washcloth and started to scrub.

The sound of raised voices made me drop the cloth and hurry to quell the escalating argument.

William stood in the doorway, soaked to the skin and dripping on the floor, while Sarah called him a coward and a bully and a few other things in what I presumed was Scottish that sounded equally uncomplimentary.

I waited for her to pause for breath before I interjected, "Sarah, it was just dirt. Nothing more." I turned my face to the light so she could see I spoke the truth. "William, why are you all wet?"

He gave me a grateful smile. "I can now say I've survived swimming with sharks." He held up his hands. "But I'll tell you both about it at dinner. After I'm out of these wet things. And not before I've kissed my wife." William winked at me and trudged to the bathroom.

Forty Seven

William cleared his throat. Sarah and I turned in our seats to see my freshly-dressed husband enter the dining room. None of us had dressed formally for dinner. Sarah said it was a waste of time and refused to go to the trouble, though I suspected she'd only brought the one evening dress and she kept that for our occasional dinner invitations with the Jacksons; so William and I…well, in his case I think it was more a matter of comfort than solidarity, though he said he would leave decisions about dinner and dress up to me, depending on my health. My morning sickness didn't show any signs of fading yet, though I'd learned I could keep it confined to the mornings if I avoided tea.

Amah ducked her head to William and disappeared into the kitchen, leaving the three of us alone.

William grinned and leaned over to kiss me. He didn't stop at a peck, either – his tongue stroked mine as his fingers gently massaged the back of my neck. I sighed blissfully, relaxing into his caress.

Sarah made a sound of disgust at our public display of affection.

William winked and captured my lips with another passionate kiss, as if inflaming his sister's ire was his intent. Maybe I should have been angry, but he'd been doing this more and more, riling her up with his less than proper behaviour in the house, and I enjoyed the absence of his grumpy façade. Not to mention the frequent kisses and contact that set my heart aflutter as if it was the first time. Perhaps it was my pregnancy that had made my love for him bloom at the slightest touch. Not to mention my raging desire, roiling beneath the surface…

Approaching footsteps made William break off the kiss and slide into his seat. "Later, lass," he murmured, as if he could read my thoughts.

Sarah shook her head, muttering about the difference between wives and drums.

Fortunately, Amah returned with a tray of food, the smell setting off my other ravenous appetite. With the evening ebb of my nausea came the desire to eat far too much and Cook delighted in providing me with food I simply couldn't resist. Tonight's roast pork was no exception — she'd seasoned it with spices that reminded me of Singapore food stalls and made my mouth water all the more.

Sarah inhaled blissfully, smiling despite her annoyance with William. She seemed to appreciate the flavours of Cook's creations almost as much as I did, which left only William to object to receiving more exotic fare than he was used to. My gaze rested on him as Amah served his meat, but William's happy smile was reserved for me. He didn't even glance at the contents of his plate or notice the drip of his damp hair soaking through his shirt collar.

My curiosity won. "William, will you tell me now why you're all wet? Where were the sharks?" And why did you swim with them without me? I added silently.

"The coolies asked for extra pay and food rations because they couldn't go fishing in the evenings. Apparently, they're scared of some huge shark that lurks at the mouth of Flying Fish Cove, stealing their catch or frightening it away. They asked Jackson first, who refused, so then they came to me."

Interesting. Despite the company hierarchy placing Jackson higher, the miners believed the real power rested with William.

William swallowed a forkful of dinner, then gulped down some wine. "I thought of refusing, too, but it was only the kampung miners asking – not the ones at South Point. So I asked them to show me the shark."

I closed my eyes, trying not to say what I was thinking. Sharks were the death of Giuseppe, my first love, and for a long time, William believed the beasts had killed me, too. How could he do something so stupid?

A warm hand landed on my arm. "I'm sorry, lass. I didn't believe there was a shark. Truly, I didn't."

I gazed into his penitent eyes and nodded.

Sarah's voice cut across our private moment, reminding us that we weren't alone. "But the shark was real?"

William chuckled. "Hold your horses, Sarah. You always wanted to skip to the end of the book when we were kids, too. Maria appreciates a good story and I'll tell it the way she likes it."

Sarah snorted but I just smiled.

After another sip of wine, William resumed, "So after work finished for today, I headed down to the cove with the coolies. Their fishing boats – kolaks, they're called, though I'd call them outrigger canoes – were all lined up on the beach, ready to go. We climbed in, two men to a boat, and paddled off out of the cove. We rounded Smith's Point and headed for what they swore was the best fishing spot along the reef. I'm surprised they didn't swear me to secrecy, too, they seemed so anxious about the spot, but never mind.

"We sat there for…oh, must have been fifteen, twenty minutes, and nothing happened. So they started setting up their fishing gear, baiting the lines and all, and lowering them over the side. It wasn't more than a couple of minutes later that a second reef rose up on the ocean side of the boat. A big, dark grey one – must've been forty feet long and six feet wide, covered in white spots that I thought were some sort of barnacle.

"Something that large…I mean, all of us

froze. They'd seen it before, but a shark that huge was bloody frightening. I thought it was a whale, but the men kept saying it was a shark and pointing to its tail. I didn't know sharks could get that enormous. I remember seeing basking sharks back home in Scotland, but the biggest of those was only half as big as this bas — er, fellow. And when he opened his mouth…it was big enough to swallow a kolak, outriggers and all. It looked like he wanted to do just that with one of them, so while he was distracted with the canoe, the men aboard leaped into the water. The shark didn't like the taste of it, though, so he turned to swallow the men instead. One of them swam away, toward another boat, but the second man just floated there, paralysed with fear.

"I didn't think. I jumped into the water after him and dragged him out of the monster's path. Just in time, too — the beast swept past, too big to turn quickly to snap us up. He must have known we were still there, though, because I felt the tail rasp against me.

Smoother than I thought, too. I thought sharks were rough, but this monster wasn't. Better for chasing after his prey, I presume.

"We just about walked on water back to the other kolaks — I heaved him over the side of the nearest one and then hauled myself back into mine. Not a moment too late, either. The monster managed to wheel around and come for another bite, but he was disappointed.

"We paddled as fast as we could back to the cove. When we were safely back on shore, the man I'd saved thanked me profusely for saving his life, offering me all sorts of things in return, but I waved him away and sent him home to his family." William grinned. "So how's that for a thrilling story, lass?"

I opened my mouth to speak, but I wasn't sure what to say. I recognised the shark species as a harmless whale shark — the only danger it posed to them was because of its size. More than anything, I was relieved. If William had swum with one of the fifteen-foot tiger sharks that made up for their lack of size with their number of teeth and skill at hunting, he wouldn't have been so lucky. He'd have died like Giuseppe.

"How could you, Will?" Sarah burst out. "You with a wife and child on the way. To risk your life for some Chinaman – "

"He was Malay and he has a wife and three children of his own. I couldn't let the shark take him," William said quietly. His eyes beseeched me.

Once again I nodded. Then I swallowed and said, "He wasn't in danger, William. A shark that big can only be a whale shark. They don't eat people or even fish. Just the coral spawn and other tiny creatures, like whales do."

William shook his head. "You didn't see it, lass. It was coming straight for him with its mouth open. I was close enough to see it had hundreds of teeth in its mouth, just waiting to chew up its dinner. That was a man-eating shark, or it would've been, if I hadn't gotten there in time." He sighed. "Tomorrow I'll have to tell Jackson to reconsider. They can't go fishing with that monster out there. And it comes to the boats, like it expects to be a fed. Someone's pet monster — someone must have been feeding it."

Me. I'd been escorting it to the densest clouds of coral spawn. The fish's presence here was my fault and it must have come looking for me. The coral had ceased spawning when we left for Singapore — the shark must be starving. I'd have to go out and tell it to go away to Cocos or Western Australia or anywhere else it could find plankton in huge quantities. But how could I speak to it if I couldn't swim out? The dolphins would spot my pregnancy instantly and summon Mother to take me home.

Unless I wasn't in the water but on top of it…

"Take me fishing," I insisted. "Take me out in one of the boats so I can show you it's harmless. We…whale sharks used to come to Cocos and we learned how to make them go away on the odd occasions they caused trouble. Maybe I can do the same here, so it will leave the fishing boats alone."

"No, lass, you can't. Think of the baby," Sarah implored.

I was thinking of my baby. Otherwise I'd head down to shore as soon as they were asleep, shift to my tail as I slipped beneath the surface and command the fish to leave and never return.

I met William's gaze squarely. His mouth was open, probably ready to deliver an entreaty just as persuasive as Sarah's, but he seemed to reconsider. He knew me better than Sarah did. "You're not getting out of the boat. I'll take you out there to see it, but once it appears, we're headed right back to shore. I won't put you in danger, lass."

I nodded. "No, I won't be in danger. Whale sharks are harmless. I'll show you."

Forty Eight

The ocean seemed to agree with Sarah, kicking up a swell that kept ships out of the cove and the kolaks firmly on the shore for over a week. For the first time in my life, I craved a calm sea. I'd never been in such a small boat before. Even my lifeboat from the *Trevessa* had been larger.

When a day dawned without surf pounding the cliffs below our house, I knew it was time.

William brought tidings of the flat sea in the cove over breakfast, but he didn't want to venture out until late afternoon, once the work day had finished, so some of the coolies could come out with us in case of a mishap. I wanted to protest William's precautions, but if it made him feel safer in the face of non-existent danger, then so be it. I didn't need guards from a whale shark and he'd soon see that.

After a day of tennis and billiards in the club, with Sarah and Anne trying to talk me out of my little sea voyage, I ensconced myself on the veranda in my sailing clothes – pants and a shirt that I'd last worn on the *Stella* with Tony at the Houtman Abrolhos.

William's face lit up when he spotted me from the road. "Perfect. Just like on the *Trevessa*, the day we were introduced. You don't look a day older, either, lass."

I remained quiet as he kissed me, but as he broke away, I said, "I hope to keep my pants on while we're on the boat this time."

To my delight, he flushed. "If you knew

what I was thinking that day, you'd have slapped me."

"You were thinking about my breasts and what you wanted to do with them," I replied. "You made squeezing motions with your hands, your pants grew tighter the longer you were with me and you adjusted my shirt to hide my curves, which made you slightly more comfortable." At his startled glance, I added, "I might not have understood what you were saying that day, but I read your body language just fine. You pulled me out of the ocean. I assume you saw everything and it was preying on your mind." I winked. "Your voice and your touch had a similar effect on me."

"Tonight, I plan to have a similar effect on you," William growled, so low that only I could hear. "After this blasted boat trip you've talked me into."

For a moment, I contemplated skipping it, and just spending the afternoon with William on land, but I'd missed the closeness of the water in my land-locked cage. What was the harm in a tiny boat trip? It's not like we'd go far at all. Just outside the cove and around the point.

William took my arm and we walked down past the port. Each person we met nodded respectfully to both of us, and I smiled in return. William's curt nods betrayed his worry, but each step brought me closer to my ocean home, buoying me up as only time in the water could. Or on the water, this time.

A ship was in port, unloading more building materials for South Point, and it looked like most of the coolie population had been conscripted into acting as lumpers to get the lumber ashore before the swell returned. The beach was empty, aside from the line of kolaks. It looked like William and I would be fishing alone without an escort.

William balked when he realised. "I'll go get some of the men from the dock," he said, starting up the beach.

"You know they have to unload that ship," I said. "I can handle a boat, William. Perhaps even better than you can. More than once I skippered a fishing boat off Fremantle. With no sail and nothing but a paddle, I'll have no problems. Help me push it into the water and get in." I leaned over to roll up my pants legs so they wouldn't get wet as we waded out.

William stared at my bare calves as if he'd never seen a woman's legs before. As if I didn't bare them every day in my most modest dresses. "I'm…I'm afraid to lose you," he said, so softly that a normal human might not have heard him.

I stretched up to lay my hand on his shoulder. "The ocean won't take me from you, I swear, William. And I can swim from the point to the beach just fine." A sudden thought struck me. "You can swim, can't you?"

He burst out laughing. "Better than you, lass, I'll wager."

I chose not to argue and tossed my shoes into the newest looking kolak. I grasped the gunwale. "On three, heave. One, two…three!" This last ended in a grunt as we shoved the boat into the water, leaving a deep groove in the sand bracketed by the tracks of the outriggers. I waded with it until the wavelets lapped at my rolled-up pants. "Right, hop in."

William stared at me. "It's always ladies first."

"You're heavier than me, so the boat will be steadier with your weight in the stern, and you're paddling, so I expect you to hold her steady with a paddle planted in the sand while I climb into the bow." I found him staring at me in wonder. "I'm sorry, William, I'm just so used to taking charge on a boat, it's like second nature. Do we have any fishing gear? It would be lovely to bring fresh fish for dinner." Not that I needed anything but my hands and my voice to catch fish, but William didn't need to know that.

"Maybe…maybe next time, lass. If you're such a mistress of seamanship as you say, we can go out every weekend, if you like." Wonder had turned to something like awe. "The number of times you've almost been lost at sea and still you don't fear it. I wish I had your courage."

I managed a smile. "I won't live my life in fear. But if we don't get going, I won't get to see your pet shark."

William gritted his teeth, nodded, and clumsily climbed into the kolak. I waited a moment for the boat to steady before I leaped in lightly after him. I settled into the bow, my face to the breeze as we set off.

The splash of William's paddle sent us slicing through the waves at surprising speed. Before I knew it, I could no longer hear the noises of the port over the lap of the waves against the kolak's hull.

When we reached the point, the wind hit me like a wall of water, plastering my shirt to my chest and whipping my hair behind me. William's chuckle made me glance behind me.

"You look like one of those figureheads on the wooden sailing ships of old," he explained. "Or a mermaid."

My smile fixed to my face, I nodded and

turned to face the wind again before he could see my stricken expression. Surely William didn't believe in mermaids, or know I was one. Mother would kill him if he did. Or I'd have to…

"Just around there is where we saw it," William shouted, pointing over my shoulder at the reefs to the west.

I nodded again. "We should use the current to take us closer. Angle the boat so it can run before the wind." A few minutes without changing direction told me that William wasn't much of a ship's navigator, so I dug out a second paddle and made the course correction myself.

"This is where we saw it," he shouted suddenly.

Yes, it was. This was precisely where I'd encountered the whale shark on my last swim. It couldn't be a coincidence — he was looking for me.

I dropped my paddle in the bottom of the boat and surveyed the waves. Its gills would allow it to stay beneath the surface indefinitely, but a hungry shark wouldn't stray far if it hoped to find me. I raised my voice to the edge of my hearing – nowhere near audible to humans – and summoned it with a song.

A familiar spotted back surfaced perhaps twenty feet away, just as large as I remembered. William's excited shout confirmed it. "That's the monster that almost ate a boat!"

"It's harmless. Nothing but a whale shark," I said. "He's just big."

"I tell you, I saw him about to eat a man!" William insisted.

Sighing, I knew there was only one way to demonstrate that the whale shark wasn't a man-eater. Or a woman-eater, either. I didn't see any dolphins nearby, so I figured I could risk it if I was quick. I gripped the gunwale and slid smoothly over the side into the water.

"NO!"

I lifted a dripping hand into the air. "Stay in the boat and watch, William." I turned my head so William wouldn't see my lips move and sang softly to the shark. It turned and altered its course to head for me and I let go of the boat, sculling with my hands to place myself in the middle of the shark's path. It opened its mouth, emitting a mournful sound that told me how hungry it was, and swam straight for me.

Forty Nine

"NO!"

A heavy weight landed on top of me, forcing me under the water so that I got an even clearer view of the whale shark's mouth full of vestigial teeth. Strong arms dragged me away as his legs kicked wildly. I wasn't sure if William was trying to kick the shark or simply swim out of its path, but his foot caught the shark a glancing blow across its snout, making it shy away.

Uncertainly, the shark cried again. I responded with the notes of a song of dismissal, telling it to swim to the distant mainland in search of food.

My head broke the surface and I realised that William had capsized our boat in his crazed leap to my aid. Half full of water, it listed heavily, as one outrigger stuck high out of the water. An audible snap of one of the connecting struts was all the warning we got before it crashed down on top of us, sending William and I back under the surface.

All I caught was a glancing blow to my arm, but William didn't move and I could see a dark trickle of blood clouding the water. Shades of Giuseppe. No. I wouldn't lose William to tiger sharks, who were undoubtedly already summoned by the blood in the water. No matter what the price. Throwing caution to the current, I raised my voice to a volume more suited to my summons, calling every dolphin within earshot. It was no request — it was a firm command that no creature in the ocean would dare disobey, even if they could.

While I waited, I dragged William to the surface, buoying him up with my own body so he could breathe freely. His eyes were closed, but he coughed and spluttered before drawing a deep lungful of air. He wasn't conscious, but he was alive, and to keep him that way I'd need the assistance of those damn dolphins. I'd eschewed a human escort, but a cetacean one was a more than able defence against sharks of the bloodthirsty kind. I dropped my face into the water, shrieking a warning to any shark in the vicinity, but the tang of blood carried further than my voice and I was already out of breath from swimming for two of us as our wet clothing threatened to drag us under again. And with my sturdy pants on, breaking out my tail would be painful as I ripped through them. So I struggled on, letting the current carry us as I waited angrily for assistance.

A cacophony of squeaks heralded their arrival, as excited dolphins spun and splashed around us in an ostentatious display. I spat out my second mouthful of water before I snapped, "*Cease playing. Carry this human safely to shore and do not let him drop below the surface or let sharks approach him from any side.*"

Subdued squeaks of assent followed as the clever creatures fashioned a sort of floating sedan chair with their bodies for William, easing him from my arms and into their conveyance. I followed behind, not even bothering to break out my gills as I stayed on the surface.

"*He is the sire of the child you carry,*" the matriarch dolphin said as she swam beside me.

I glanced at her. "*Yes. And precious to me, so anyone who harms him will —*"

"*Elder Sephira is near. She searches for you and will have heard your call.*"

I stared at the dolphin. If Mother was nearby and knew about my baby, all my efforts had been for nothing. My cage had busted wide open and my catty mother could enter at will.

I watched the dolphins carry William through the waves to the shore, then leave him on the sand as they helped each other back into the water. He'd be safe for the moment, but I'd need to take him higher up the sand so the tide wouldn't reach him. If my mother knew of him, and wanted him dead, it wouldn't be enough.

I needed to silence the gossip before it started – and for that I needed the dolphin matriarch's help. I scrutinised the dolphin at my side. She had the slight somnolence I recognised from other creatures I'd controlled with a song. Did that mean she was more under my control than my mother's? There was only one way to find out.

"I do not wish her to know about this human. There will be no gossip about him," I commanded.

"As you wish, Sirena. She does not care for humans. Just you and the child you carry." The dolphin swam serenely on.

My heart froze. Had I sacrificed my freedom and my daughter's for William's life?

If I had, it was a fitting price to pay for the life of the man I loved.

I splashed ashore beside him, then dragged him up the beach along a track that looked like it had been made by a sea turtle. Wishing I had the energy to worry about the future, I slumped to the sand beside him. Huddled up to his wet body, I sank into sleep.

Fifty

Something pinched my toe, as if trying to determine what it was. I let out a string of swearing that sent the crab scuttling back. No, not just one – they all retreated to a form a rough circle around us, leaving two feet of bare sand between my body and them.

"What did you say, lass?" William opened bleary eyes and stared at me.

"Probably nothing polite," I responded with

a rueful smile. I touched his head, where a gash had oozed enough blood to make his hair matted on one side. "Are you all right?"

"It hurts, but I'll be fine. How'd we get here?" He surveyed the empty…no, almost empty beach. While we'd slept, a half-dozen green turtles had joined us, varying in size from a foot across to a couple of three-foot creatures who were older than my mother.

I didn't think he'd believe me if I told him the truth. "I swam us here." I managed to smile. "Dragging you up the beach was even harder, but I wasn't sure how high the tide would get."

William chuckled. "You mean to say you saved my life again? I swore I'd protect you, yet here you are, my courageous little heroine of a wife. I should show you just how grateful I am…" The glint in his eye was unmistakeable, sparking my desire, too.

"I only got us to shore. I'm not sure how far back the cove and the Settlement are from here, because I don't know which beach this is," I admitted.

William eyed the cliffs above us. "West White Beach, to the west of Margaret and Rhoda Beaches. One of the most inaccessible spots on the island without a boat, but here we are. And no boat." Now his smile looked forced. "It's too far to swim, lass. But everyone in the cove saw us leave. They'll send a boat out after us or maybe even the cargo ship, if they don't find us right away. All we have to do is wait, and I have a few ideas for what we could do while we wait."

I surrendered to his kisses, happy to help him out of his shirt to see if he had any other injuries I didn't know about. He slipped a hand into my pants, eliciting a moan from my lips before I tried to take the pants off entirely.

A deep, bass throbbing began in the distance and William's skilful fingers deserted me. I started to protest, but William laid a salty finger across my lips. "We're saved," he said softly.

We lay on the sand, scanning the horizon as

the cargo ship steamed into view from the west. It must have circled the whole island. It proceeded slowly, as close to shore as its deep draught would allow, and I could see men at the railing, scanning the shore. Searching for us.

William rose, grabbed his shirt and started waving it above his head like a flag, shouting at the top of his lungs. I clambered to my feet more slowly, wondering whether I should do the same or fasten the buttons of my shirt, which had mysteriously come undone.

The cargo ship cruised closer and dropped anchor just offshore, signalling that they'd seen us as they lowered a launch. Four men manned it, rowing far faster than William and I had in our kolak. As I watched their approach, I caught a glimpse of something shimmering between the waves breaking against the ship's hull. For a moment, I thought it was the morning sun reflecting off the water, but this was in the ship's shadow. I looked harder and glimpsed her again — a tail fluke this time.

Definitely deep blue, but with a gold sheen that I knew all too well. Mother lurked offshore, ready to snatch me up the moment I got close enough.

I straightened so I stood at my full height, facing the threat head-on. If she wanted me, she'd have to take me against my will and in front of a shipload of human witnesses…and I wouldn't lift a fin to help her.

I was so intent on Mother that I barely noticed the launch had reached the shallows. The men aboard beckoned to us. William scooped me up in his arms and carried me to the boat, for all the world as if he'd saved me and not the other way around. I didn't mind – this might be the last time I felt his warm embrace and I wanted to remember it. If these were our last moments together, his life was worth the sacrifice. Worth everything.

The lighter clanged against the ship, jolting me out of my morbid thoughts as the cargo ship's crew winched us aboard. After what seemed like an eternity banging up the side, the lighter swung around and landed on the deck with one final, jarring bump. William lifted me out, his feet thumping onto the solid cargo ship's deck. I didn't take my eyes off Mother for a moment, expecting her to try and sink the ship. As I watched her inaction, I realised that I was mistaken. I could sink this ship, driving those aboard to insanity and violence with a song, but her voice lacked the power to do so. The one time we'd both sought to control Tony, I had won. She could control a human as well as any siren...but only if I didn't fight her. And I'd fight for William with my last breath.

"Don't cry, lass. We're safe now," he said, and I realised that my tears had spilled down my cheeks, blurring my vision.

The ship weighed anchor and I lost sight of Mother in our wake as we steamed back to the cove. Manoeuvring the ship into its old mooring against the pier took considerable time and more than once I caught my fingers drumming against the railing in impatience.

Every moment spent docking was time Mother would swim to catch up. And she wouldn't let me slip through her fingers again.

When William helped me off the gangplank, I risked a glance at the water. Mother's eyes met mine from the shadows under the pier. A long moment passed before she bowed her head and sank beneath the surface.

"No more fishing for you, lass. No more boats for me, either," William said, setting me down on the shore.

"No. I don't think I'll be spending much time on the ocean at all, at least until after the birth." I patted my belly, feeling the tiny flutter as the child inside reminded me of her presence.

"We're safe now."

Safe. Perhaps.

A dark blue tail broke the surface at the entrance to the cove.

But for how long?

ABOUT THE AUTHOR

Demelza Carlton has always loved the ocean, but on her first snorkelling trip she found she was afraid of fish.

She has since swum with sea lions, sharks and sea cucumbers and stood on spray drenched cliffs over a seething sea as a seven-metre cyclonic swell surged in, shattering a shipwreck below.

Demelza now lives in Perth, Western Australia, the shark attack capital of the world.

The *Ocean's Gift* series was her first foray into fiction, followed by her suspense thriller *Nightmares* trilogy. She swears the *Mel Goes to Hell* series ambushed her on a crowded train and wouldn't leave her alone.

Want to know more? You can follow Demelza on Facebook, Twitter, YouTube or her website, Demelza Carlton's Place at:

www.demelzacarlton.com

Books by Demelza Carlton

Siren of Secrets series

Ocean's Secret (#1)
Ocean's Gift (#2)
Ocean's Infiltrator (#3)

Siren of War series

Ocean's Justice (#1)
Ocean's Widow (#2)
Ocean's Bride (#3)
Ocean's Rise (#4)
Ocean's War (#5)
How To Catch Crabs

Nightmares Trilogy

Nightmares of Caitlin Lockyer (#1)
Necessary Evil of Nathan Miller (#2)
Afterlife of Alana Miller (#3)

Mel Goes to Hell series

The Devil's Work (#1)
See You in Hell (#2)
Mel Goes to Hell (#3)
To Hell and Back (#4)
The Holiday From Hell (#5)
All Hell Breaks Loose (#6)
The Devil Goes to Heaven (#7)

9 781925 799293